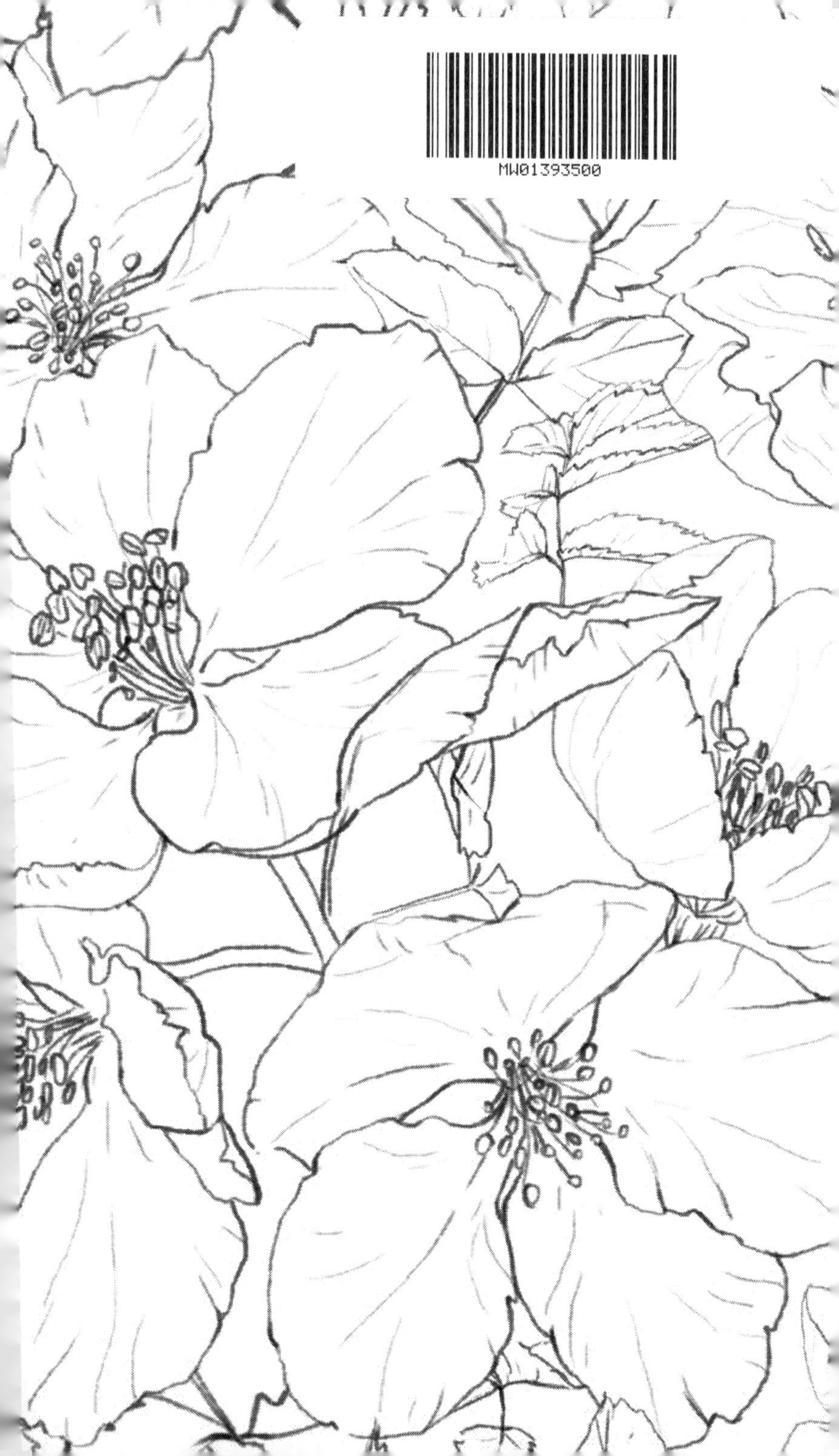

No part of this publication may be reproduced, stored in a retrieval system, or transmitted in any form or by any means, electronic, mechanical, photocopying, recording, scanning, or otherwise, without the prior written permission of the publisher, except in the case of brief quotations within critical reviews and otherwise as permitted by copyright law.

NOTE: This is a work of fiction. Names, characters, places, and incidents are a product of the author's imagination. Any resemblance to real life is purely coincidental. All characters in this story are 18 or older.

Copyright © 2018, Willow Winters Publishing. All rights reserved.

Nathan
&
Harlow

Willow Winters
Wall street journal & usa today bestselling author

From USA Today bestselling author Willow Winters comes a emotionally gripping, standalone, contemporary romance.

Nathan always had the most beautiful smile.
Every time I caught a glimpse of it, I had to smile too.
It didn't matter that he grew up on the wrong side of the city,
I saw the good in him… even when he didn't.

That wasn't enough to keep us together in high school though.
One night ruined everything. A night I'll never forget.

Years have passed and now he's on the cover of magazines and the star of movies.
The reformed bad boy with a charming smile who makes women weak in the knees.
No one knows what happened that night that forced us apart.
No one can ever know.
The moment he locked his light blue eyes on me again, I was ruined.

I never stood a chance.

SECOND CHANCE

Prologue

Harlow

10 YEARS AGO
APRIL

The red, white, and bright blue lights reflect off the large glass windows of the liquor store. The sirens have stopped. I swear they were only screaming in my ear for a split second. They were loud enough to make my heart leap into my throat and send fear flowing freely through my blood.

They were silenced quickly, as if turned on by mistake.

I swear it was all an accident.

"Nathan." I say his name weakly, searching his cold gaze as I grip his wrists. My nails dig in as my throat goes dry. He doesn't answer me, doesn't give me a minute to ask questions. He merely blocks me from the view of the police car pulling up to the curb.

His back is to the cops and he doesn't turn to face them, even as the sound of the cruiser's window rolling down drowns out the sound of my blood rushing in my ears.

Nathan leans closer to me as my shoulder and ass hit the unyielding wall of the liquor store. His dark eyes look even darker and the lack of any emotion on his face forces my plea for him to tell me how to make this right to catch in my throat. "Don't say a word," he hisses in my ear.

One second, one beat of my heart passes feeling caught in an eternity as I look up into the eyes of the boy I thought I loved. The boy I thought loved me back. "Don't be stupid, Hally," he says low, beneath his breath.

But I never really knew him, did I?

The boy I knew wasn't capable of this.

But it was only an accident.

"Nathan, we have to-" I try to speak, but the words are silenced as he narrows his eyes. The shadows from the dim street lights make the sharp lines of his jaw look even more intense.

"You two alright?" I hear a man say from behind us, but my eyes don't break away from Nathan's. It's the cops. So close. So close to knowing everything that just happened only minutes ago.

Nathan's the first to break. He lets go of my forearm and turns his back to me, leaving the chill of the night to turn the thin sheen of sweat on my skin to ice. I wrap my arms around my chest and as I do, I see a small bit of blood on my arm and then more. Just a large scrape I think, but I'm quick to hide it. As fast as I can, I pull the thin sleeves of my sweater down my arms. It's evidence.

"We're fine," Nathan says, although I almost don't hear him. My heart beats harder and faster; I'm desperate to escape as I stand on legs that quiver, legs too afraid to do anything.

"And you, miss?" the cop says as a bright light flashes in front of me. The sudden light causes me to wince and then look up at him. The dark blue of his uniform looks black in the low light. The man is older with salt and pepper hair, and looks experienced and wise enough to know a lie. I don't trust my voice, so I simply nod and almost cross my arms again, but then I remember the blood and my fingers grip the hem of my sweater to keep my arms at my sides.

"You two look a little young to be out here," the cop says, his eyes flickering from mine to Nathan's.

We're in high school. Nathan's a year older than me and a senior this year.

"Are you from around here?" the cop asks and I'm not sure who he's talking to, but Nathan answers for us both.

His thin Henley pulls tight over his broad shoulders as he points his thumb behind him. "She's from the Hills and I'm down here."

The cop's jaw goes tense, his eyes burning into me but I don't look back at him.

I'm not supposed to be here. I hear it before the words even come from his mouth.

I ignore everything that the cop says; I'm not interested in being told where I belong. The only thing I can concentrate on is my ability to breathe. I feel like I'm being suffocated. If I had just listened, none of this would have happened. I already know it's true and that makes the guilt so much worse.

"Can you take her home?" I hear Nathan ask and it's as if that's what they were waiting for. How could he? After what just happened, I'm shaking and fear is still raw and coursing through my blood. How could he leave me after that? Tears prick my eyes as I will him to justify it.

But I already know the answer; it's my fault. I should have stuck to my usual routine and not taken the wrong way home. The way that leads to nothing but trouble.

I don't care though. I'm scared. I can't leave him; I can't be by myself. I try to scream out, I try to grip his arm, but he whips around before I can do a damn thing and the heat in his eyes is something I never expected to see.

The anger. So much anger.

"I didn't mean it," I whimper out of instinct and then pray the cops didn't hear. Please. He has to know I never wanted this. I never knew it would come to this. Please. Please, God, let me take it back. "I'm sorry." The words crack as I say them.

"I already told you we were over," Nathan says in such a deep voice, rough and riddled with accusations. The guilt pounds through my veins, heating my blood and sending a shame through me that makes me sick.

"We have to ..." I start to tell him we need to confess. We have to tell the cops what happened.

"We don't have to do a damn thing and you better not say shit," Nathan says with a thinly-veiled threat. *"Get in that car,"* Nathan says with certainty and conviction, and I lose all sense of composure.

"Don't ever come back, Hally," Nathan says as I cover my mouth and keep the sobs from coming up. *"I won't tell you again,"* he says beneath his breath, ignoring how my world is shattered and my body just wants to collapse and give in to the pain.

I didn't mean for this to happen. If I could just go back in time.

The night is disturbed by the slam of the police car door and a second officer gets out of the car, stopping Nathan as he tries to leave. I can barely hear what they're saying and I try to go to him. I will my legs to move, but the first officer is quick to grab my arm. I rip it away from him and stumble back, tripping over my feet and nearly falling as I look up at him, bewildered.

"It's alright," the cop says easily, just now realizing how startled I am and I can't help but notice the look he gives Nathan as if he's to blame. *He has no idea.*

"I need you to come with me," the officer says with a stern voice, no negotiation apparent in his tone. *As if he already knows the truth.*

Nathan turns to look back at me, but his jaw is clenched and the other officer is quick to get his attention again. Speaking low, in whispers, so I can't hear. I can only see Nathan shake his head.

I stare at Nathan as the officer talks, willing him to look at me as I'm pulled away from the street. I can't hear a word, not from the officer leading me away and not from the officer speaking to Nathan. My shoes click on the sidewalk, the cold night air making each breath hurt more and more.

It's almost like everything's happening in slow motion. It seems to last an eternity. Each detail captured clearly.

With every second that passed, I could have said something. With every second I could have apologized.

But before I knew it, he was walking away, and I was being driven in the opposite direction.

I stare out of the window, tears burning my eyes as he disappears from view. The dark night only illuminated by a street light and the bright neon glow of a bar. I keep my eyes on the cracked concrete sidewalk rather than look up at the people leaning against the brick wall of the building as we slowly come to a stop at a red light.

"Are you alright, miss?" the cop asks me again, turning in his seat to face me, but I don't have the decency to look him in the eyes as I lie.

No. I'm not okay. I'll never be okay.

But no one can know.

It was ten years ago and although that night should have traumatized me for an entirely different reason, the fact that I listened to Nathan and didn't come forward is what haunts me.

It's a funny thing, fate. Life goes on day after day and I didn't notice how all the pieces were lining up like dominoes.

I tried to smile as the weeks turned into months and months turned into years, thinking I'd left my past behind me. I thought I knew what was going on around me. I thought I'd survived and had a new life, with the truth of that night being buried ten feet under.

But fate put me where I'm standing right now.

Fate's the reason the dominoes are falling, crashing into my reality and leaving me shattered.

It's so easy to blame fate. But I don't have any other explanation.

Nathan didn't plan this, and neither did I.

It's a funny thing, fate. It loves to fuck you over.

Chapter 1

Harlow

"Holy shit," I say, the words slipping out under my breath. I barely hear them myself. I swallow thickly and then wipe my sweaty palms on my plum pencil skirt. A gust of wind blowing along East Fifty-fifth Street causes my loose cream blouse to billow and sends a chill down my heated skin.

I barely feel it though, as I stand here feeling like a fraud.

I've always been a normal girl with a normal life. Everything happened so quickly and I just kept nodding my head in disbelief. And now I'm here. Standing outside of the St. Gerard hotel. It's a sleek and modern building made of black glass and shiny steel. It's full of a hustle and bustle that echoes the busy streets of New York, but with an edge and sophistication that doesn't allow for outsiders. It's high end and only meant for the who's who of New York City.

And I'm expected to walk through those doors. Just a girl from the suburbs who always dreamed of getting an inch closer to the city.

My heart races thinking about holding my head up high and squaring my shoulders, pretending like I belong here. There's only so much a person can fake and right now, I can't even pretend to have confidence. *Fake it till you make it.* I say the motto over and over. It's worked for me so far.

"I know, right?" Lydia says with a different air to her tone than mine. Not quite disbelief, more like the sound of accomplishment. The voice someone uses when they know they've made it and they're damn proud.

Sometimes, I wonder at what point she went from being my first client at the agency to a friend. Since day one, only months ago, the air between us has been easy and she's only shown me a sweet side that's made it easy to confide in her. Today, of all days, I need someone to lean on and to ground me. I couldn't have lucked out more.

"Like, ho-ly shit," I say each syllable separately, thankful that she's hell-bent on keeping me from making an utter fool of myself.

This is my first real time on set, even though I've been interning with one of the top talent agents in Manhattan for months. This is my first time at a real shoot. Well, maybe not today, but sometime in the next few weeks. Not that I wanted this. I never asked for it and a happy accident led me here. It's Lydia's fault. *The bitch set me up.* A smile slips onto my face at the thought.

Lydia was made to be a star, with high cheekbones and straight black hair that's never needed a keratin blowout. She's going to kill it in there and earn her place in this industry. She's *supposed* to be here.

"We got this," she says as she maneuvers the Louis Vuitton bag onto her shoulder and smacks her lips together, but the stain doesn't budge on her lips.

"I don't know if I can do this," I say softly, my eyes traveling along the etched glass sign above the doorway. My gaze follows the glass elevator as it moves seamlessly up the 150-story building until my eyes can't focus on it anymore. The glare of the sun forces me to slip my sunglasses back into place. I feel sick to my stomach.

Lydia just smiles, her bright red lips thinning as her pearly whites flash back at me. "You know those aren't your lines, right?" she asks and then glides the tip of her tongue across her teeth and steps forward, ignoring the dozens of people hurrying to move around us as if we don't even exist. She's not intimidated by the building, the people, *or* the expectations we're about to walk into.

Ever since high school, almost ten years ago now, I've thought about what it would be like to be an actress. I didn't dare to really dream of it though. I thought I could do casting calls or learn to be an agent. Something in the industry, but I never hoped to actually participate on screen. My first summer out of college as an intern proved this industry moves fast and I need to be prepared for anything.

"Four weeks of this," Lydia says as a woman in a chic pink Chanel tweed dress and a thin black patent leather belt around her waist walks past us. It's hard not to notice her. Her hot pink pumps click loudly on the sidewalk, and even with the traffic and other people moving about, she stands out as a force that refuses to blend in. She walks right ahead of us, a large Dooney and Bourke purse in the crook of her arm and the doors open without hesitation, allowing her entry.

My heart flips once, then twice, as my legs turn to jello and she disappears beyond the black glass. Lydia mumbles something incoherently, gripping my arm and making me nearly topple over. "That was Julie Rays! Julie!" she squeals.

I stare back at her, bewildered. I should know that name. I should know everyone on set. It was my job at the agency to know anyone worth knowing in this industry. But for the life of me, my mind is blank. I force a smile and nod my head as Lydia gathers her composure. Her smile is infectious; her confidence, her everything.

Julie Rays. I say her name in my head over and over. "Oh, shit. Julie Rays." It finally clicks and my eyes widen as I search beyond the glass for her figure, but she's gone. Julie's an up-

and-coming actress. The star of not one, but two new top-rated shows on television last year. I should have recognized her in a heartbeat. She's one of the hottest actresses right now and she just walked past me only a few feet away.

"Oh my God, do you think she's on the same set?" I ask Lydia, who lets a sly smile slip onto her face. We don't know a single thing about the stars of the show. To control publicity, NDAs are standard before shooting begins.

"Don't leave me," I tell Lydia as she starts to move toward the building. The request comes out in a single breath and more like a desperate question than anything else.

"There's no way I'm letting you go anywhere without me," she says with a wink and pulls me toward the doors. Lydia doesn't even break her stride as the doorman pulls the all-glass door wide open and tips his head to greet her.

My feet move in unison with Lydia's pace as I take in the expansive lobby. The high ceilings make the ambient sounds echo in the large room. To the right side is an open-concept restaurant and I only take a quick glance. There are high-end shops on my left and an enormous fountain in the very center. Just beyond, there's a large mahogany desk that spans the length of the open lobby. The reception desk. Right where we're headed.

One of the four women behind the desk looks up at us with a smile, her platinum blonde hair pulled back tightly into a high bun. Everyone in here oozes wealth and sophistication.

"You're fine," Lydia whispers to me and her voice makes me turn to her. "If you could stop gripping me like you're about to float away, I'd appreciate it," she says.

I instantly let go of her arm.

It's just that ... I'm intimidated. There's no other way to put it. I'm terrified I'm going to fail. That I'll ruin this once-in-a-lifetime opportunity.

"You're seriously going to do fine," Lydia says, practically reading my mind as we come to a stop in front of the desk.

Before I can even utter a response, she's already moved on and is giving our names to the receptionist, Alexis, or so it says on the shiny silver tag above her shirt pocket.

"And how can I help you, Miss Parker?"

"We're here for filming with Mr. Stevens," Lydia says and adds, "The fifteenth floor, I believe." Her soft smile and elegance speak of confidence and certainty. Sure enough, the receptionist nods and reveals key cards, swiping them in something I can't fully see next to her computer.

I swallow the lump in my throat and look around the large lobby, watching as the men and women, each dressed in varying degrees of wealth, move across the tiled marble. The ceiling is domed and so high I have to crane my neck to see the etched designs along the coffered ceiling.

I wonder if they can tell I'm a girl from outside the city. One of the ones who stares out of her window at night and memorizes each building that's lit up off in the distance. No one special, and destined to stay in the same town where I grew up.

My mother insisted that a college degree wasn't necessary. She loved having me work with her in the corner shop selling secondhand antiques and collectibles. I did it for years, but going to school was a chance to get closer to the bright lights of the city. Every year inching nearer, but knowing within four short years I'd be right back in the suburbs, working at my mom's shop and making her proud.

One day, I'm just a marketing student. The next, I'm taking an internship under Nancy Welsh, a well-known agent.

I shouldn't have applied; all it did was upset my mother, who didn't understand, and pulled me closer to a life I didn't think I was supposed to lead.

Within two weeks, I was practicing line readings with a client and up-and-coming actress, Lydia Parker, sweet and seemingly unassuming. But Lydia is cunning, and she knows the ways of this industry. It wasn't an accident that we were practicing lines in the coffee shop that the director, Stevens, frequented. What Lydia wants, Lydia gets.

I guess him catching sight of me makes me a happenstance of sorts. I'm just a minor character, but still, it's more than I ever thought I'd be.

I almost turn my head, tearing my eyes away from the abstract stone sculptures on either side of the elevator when I hear Lydia thank the receptionist. I almost carry on, allowing myself to move through the motions of something I only dared to imagine.

But my eyes catch sight of a man as he enters an elevator. His thin, brown, worn leather jacket is pulled tightly across his broad shoulders as he walks.

My heart stops beating. The chatter and faint sounds turn to white noise. *It can't be him.* I tell myself over and over. My lips part and I nearly take a step forward, mostly from disbelief. My hand instantly reaches behind me for Lydia, but I'm not aware if it's even her. I just need something to grab onto in order to stay grounded.

I recognize him by the way he moves. The way his hand slips into the back pocket of his dark blue jeans and pulls out the necessary card. I know it's him before he even turns around. The sharp jawline is new, accompanying an older version of the boy I used to know. But his eyes I would know anywhere. The darkness that swirls, the chill in his gaze, yet the heat it brings me. They hold me captive, make me weak, make me crave the way things were before I lost him.

Nathan Hart.

There's a secret, a dark past between us. Something I've tried to ignore and pretend never happened. It's what tore us apart and even though I've accepted what occurred and my part in it, I don't think I'll ever be okay.

Time is a bitch. It slows and seems to stay still, refusing to move or to let me respond with anything but disbelief. I wish I hadn't been looking toward the elevator doors as they start to close, taking him away from me. But I am and as they slowly close, his eyes drift to mine. I'm caught in his stare. Unmoving and trapped by fate as his eyes widen slightly with recognition.

Then time continues, sure that I've seen him and he's seen me, certain that it's destroyed me in this moment. And I'm released, turning from the doors as quickly as I can.

He wasn't supposed to be here.

But I know I saw him and he saw me.

And that changes everything.

Chapter 2

Nathan

I don't think my blood can get any colder. My jaw and every other muscle in my body are tense. This is exactly why I didn't want to leave Los Angeles. The ghosts follow me everywhere.

The reminders of what I left behind.

But the vision of her was so real.

Her pale lips and the curve of her neck and shoulders. I can practically feel her soft skin against the tips of my fingers. I close my eyes as the elevator dings and everyone in the spacious cart shifts forward, ready to move before the doors have even begun to open.

My body refuses to be anything but tightly wound, not wanting to believe it was her, but unable to deny it.

I'd know her anywhere, even if it has been nearly a decade. The way her doe eyes stared straight into me, unlike anyone else can. Cutting through me and holding me still. It has to be her.

My Hally.

Older and looking back at me with something akin to fear. And I know why. I may have loved her, but she kept pushing and pushing. My hands clench into white-knuckled fists. The people move but I keep my pace even and my stride casual as I exit the elevator. I nearly look around the room, lost and confused as to why I'm here and forgetting who I am. Why I'm heading past rows of stage equipment and lighting.

I barely notice the glances and knowing smiles as I make my way back. Refusing to look flustered or as though I'm off balance in the least. I just need to get to my dressing room. It's here somewhere and then I can lock everyone out and get a grip.

She wasn't supposed to be here. Out of everyone in New York, what is *she* doing here?

"Mr. Hart," Stevens, the director, says from the back corner of the stage to my right. The backdrop goes all the way up the twelve-foot-high ceilings, although the paint itself stops before the plywood reaches the top of the wall. It's fitted with everything needed to look as though it's a living room. It's all the same here, and I only focus on doing my job.

Well, not *here*. Not in television shows.

LA is where I've been since I left Bailey, a town about two hours away from NYC. Since the day an agent met me outside of prison and told me he'd change my life forever. He was right and I never looked back.

Movies are out and TV shows are in, or so my agent says. And like the good client I am, I took his advice and came out here even though it was so close to *her*. I should have known better than to return anywhere close to where I grew up. I've been on edge ever since I got on that plane to come back here. I thought I'd be hours away. Hours from Hally and everyone else I left behind. As if there was ever enough space to make me forget.

"There he is," my agent, Mark, practically yells out, clapping his hands once as he pushes off from the stage wall near the row of dressing rooms and walks over to me. His suit is crisp and impeccably tailored.

I halt in my tracks; my eyes are drawn to the sign on the door behind him. The one with my name embossed on a gold star. The room I know I can disappear into.

I try to loosen my coiled muscles and greet Mark Shannon. I owe him everything and he deserves that much. But I can't shake the knowledge that she was right there. My skin heats. *She saw me.*

And she didn't come to me.

My heart drops at the thought and I barely register what Mark's saying. I've never stopped wanting her and seeing her so close is too much to just let her slip away.

"Line readings at two and then you need to be on set no later than three," Mark starts with the schedule. I'm sure he has it all memorized, although he's got a stack of papers in his left hand. His right hand grabs my shoulder as he guides me to the door, rattling off names and times that I don't give a shit about.

He opens the door for me and pushes it forward, not stopping to even take a breath. He moves at a mile a minute and I let him. It doesn't matter if I even respond, so long as I sign my name on the dotted line and I always do.

I take a look around and everything's familiar. These rooms are all the same. A bed, a desk, a makeup vanity. They're all solid wood and decorated nicely although it's made to be temporary and that's more than obvious by the quick construction.

I always tell Mark, modern. I'm not quite sure what it means, but the rooms always come with enough to keep me occupied and comfortable for the first few days. And then I get antsy.

It used to make Mark squirm and get nervous when I'd leave the set. Especially when he first brought me on, taking a risk on the boy from New York with a bad rep but the talent and looks to make headlines in production. *Bad boy turned movie star.* He doesn't give a shit anymore though. Like I said, I show up, do my job and get back to where I belong. Alone.

The small fridge opening catches my attention. I turn to see Mark bending down and listen to the sound of glasses clinking against one another.

He pulls out two bottles of pale ale and holds them up for me to see. "Just like you like it," he says confidently.

I couldn't care less about beer right now. I feel like a dick as I watch Mark take in my posture, as it slowly dawns on him that I'm completely uninterested.

I'm grateful. I really am. He found me the day I walked out of prison, at only nineteen years old. He gave me a life I don't deserve and I hate that he's looking at me as though I'm anything but happy for all he's done.

"You name it, Nate," he tells me, walking forward and putting the bottles down on the desk next to the fridge.

The words are caught in my throat, but her name is all I can think to say. The only explanation I can give.

His face is deadly serious as he stands right in front of me, nearly a foot shorter and looks me straight in the eyes. "You name it and I'll get it here in no time."

My teeth grind; my pride and something else, fear maybe, want me to shut the fuck up and just tell him everything's fine.

But I'm desperate. And desperate men do foolish things.

"There's a girl," I start and then clear my throat. "A woman."

Mark stares at me, waiting for more and ready to deliver. "Harlow May." Her name is like a sin on my tongue. So sweet and tempting. The sound warms my chest and just saying her name brings a sense of peace about me. The anxiousness leaves me slowly as he nods.

"Harlow May," he says and nods repeatedly, although his eyes stayed glued to mine.

"She was here in the lobby," I tell him and my blood heats

remembering how she looked at me. The fear in her eyes was the very same that was there when I last saw her. When I told her to stay away and never speak to me again.

"Alright, she was here and you want to ...?" Mark questions and it pisses me off.

"I want to know why. I want to know everything about her," I say and my voice comes out firm and absent of negotiation. I'm fully aware of how fucked up my request is. "I want her here," I add. I don't give a shit if it's crazy. I couldn't give a damn what he thinks. "Just make it happen," I tell him words I hear these assholes tell their agents all the time. I've never requested anything from Mark, ever, but I need this. *I need to know if it was really her.*

"She wasn't in the pilot, so if she is here, she's no one important," Mark says easily and then seems to think twice about his word choice. Maybe it's because my eyes narrow and that uneasiness I've been trying to shake comes back full force.

"Give me five minutes," he says as he starts walking briskly to the door. "I'll know exactly who she is, where she is, what she's doing, and who she's fucking in five minutes," he says and then flinches when my eyes flash with anger.

"I don't want to know who she's fucking," I spit back at him and then regret it. Not because of how pissed off I sound, but because it's a lie. I do want to know. I close my eyes and run a hand down my face in frustration as my head throbs while I listen to the door opening and closing.

I know she wasn't in the pilot. He didn't have to tell me that.

One episode down, and five to go for this season. If things go well and the show gets picked up for the next season, then ten episodes are tentatively slated for season two. Even starring in so many damn episodes, the shooting time is only thirty days. Television production is proving much faster than cinema.

Which means fewer days with her. If she's even here for the show. I try to ignore the hope I feel at seeing her again. I try to ignore the way my stomach churns at the thought of being close to her again.

Hally was a mistake all those years ago. She brought chaos to my life. A torrent of emotion I thrived on, a tension between the two of us that I was addicted to. I know it was the same for her. The two of us together was nothing but destructive. Both of us tearing at each other, even if it was only to get closer. Desperate for one another in every way.

If she's here, I'm fucked. I already know that much.

I'm on edge as I open up the door to my room and stand there, watching everyone move about and praying for a distraction. The fourteenth and fifteenth floors are booked for production. Different sets on each and our rooms are scattered throughout the building.

My eyes drift from one person to the next, each on a cell phone or getting their makeup done or preparing in some way for the long days ahead of us. It's showbiz and it moves a mile a minute. Or at least it does around me.

I used to be eager for this. To play a role that someone else chose and fade into a life that wasn't my own. Even if it was just for a moment. I could be someone else and forget my own name. Forget where I grew up and how I had no one. Forget how I ran away from the one person who had ever made me feel anything but anger.

Scripts and gigs were easy to become consumed with; I was that desperate to be anyone besides the person I'd become. And not a damn thing could stop me from playing the part Mark gave me. I wasn't bred for this lifestyle, but after years of being shoved in front of cameras and taking over the spotlight, nothing fazes me anymore.

But knowing she's here somewhere in this building, or was ... She may have already left.

The realization makes my blood spike with adrenaline, and the need to run to her and stop her from getting any further is sobering.

I didn't want to lose her. I didn't want to walk away. But that's the way it had to happen. Life decided that, not me. I never thought I'd see her face again. I've been running from her for years.

Chapter 3

Harlow

You're going to do great, sweetheart. Break a leg!

I stare down at the text from my father and I can't even reply. He's so damn proud of me and I know he chuckled when he typed up that second line. But my lips are unmoving and in a grim line.

My butt is firmly planted on Lydia's bed by the desk in her room, laptop open and script in hand. I haven't budged from my spot in her room, but I know this is temporary.

I have to go out there. Any minute now, I need to get up and face him.

Nathan's name is in bold lettering on the first page of the screenplay. Mine is in tiny print toward the very end. Mostly on the second to last page. I need to suck it up and prepare myself for the inevitable. I've had two days to try to figure out what to do and get a grip.

No one told me who was in this production when I signed up for it. No one warned me that the one person on the face of the earth who hates me was going to be here. Yet I can't bring myself to turn around and walk away. I keep telling myself it's a once-in-a-lifetime opportunity; that I won't let him ruin it for me. Or let the past haunt me like it did for years.

But the truth is that I *want* to see him more than anything else. I never wanted to say goodbye to him, but he shoved me away when I needed him most.

I know he's here. Now that filming's begun, I'm well aware of the fact I'm on the same floor as he is. I don't know if he knows I'm here. He saw me, I'm sure of it. But he hasn't come searching for me. He hasn't had me fired either. So maybe that's a start.

The only thing I really know is that I'm desperate to get one more look at him. I'm desperate to see him in person again and not just in the trailers for movies I refuse to watch. I'm scared to death, but I need to hear him say my name again.

Not enough to leave Lydia's dressing room, though. Chickenshit is what I am. But at least I haven't run.

Ten years ago
March 6

I want to get up out of this seat before the bell goes off, but I have to wait. Class is over and the sound of everyone packing their geography books and notebooks back into their backpacks along with chatter and laughter surround me. But it's all just white noise.

My breath comes in shallow pants as I peek over at Nathan and find him staring at me.

I'm quick to rip my eyes away from him and focus on shoving my textbook into my bag. It won't fit and I find myself shoving it harder and harder and getting more and more pissed off. I know I'm taking out my frustrations on the damn over packed bookbag, but at least it's an outlet.

I hate him. I hate Nathan for what he said last night. I hate that we're on-again, off-again. I hate that I gave myself to him. Each thought accompanies a shove until the stupid book is in place and I have to zip up the bag.

I mostly hate him for letting me go so easily. For making it clear that I'm not to him what he is to me. That's the part I hate the most. I hate I gave so much of myself to him. The bell goes off, and I tear my eyes from the bag then look up to the clock above the door.

Shit. I wanted to be the first out. I wanted to beat him and get away from him. Fuck it. I'll let him leave first then. I collapse into the seat, leaving the bag on the floor and slipping my thumb under my bra strap that fell down my arm, hiking it back up. Staring straight ahead, I ignore everyone, all of the students filing out and look fixedly at the blackboard. Mr. Jones' chicken scratch of whatever he was talking about today is still there. I didn't hear a damn word, not that it matters. All his tests are based on the quizzes in the back of every chapter.

The sounds get softer and softer as the room empties and I try not to watch the door. I won't watch him leave; I refuse to give him that satisfaction.

The sound of sneakers scuffing against the floor to my left forces me to look. I keep my head down, but I recognize his jeans, his shoes. I know it's him and it makes my heart sink into the pit of my stomach. I cried all night and I don't want to cry here. Even if the only person left in this damn room is Mr. Jones.

"You want me to get it?" Nathan asks me and I have to look up, confused by what he means.

"Your bag?" he clarifies and I don't know how to answer. I can't keep doing this back and forth. I can't be friends with an ex. Not the two of us. I love him too much to just be friends.

I shake my head, not trusting myself to speak. My voice feels raw and I can feel the tears pricking, threatening to spill over.

It's when he tosses my bag over his shoulder and holds his hand out for me to take that the splintered pieces in my chest seem to warm, growing hotter and hotter until I place my hand in his and stand up in the small space he's given me. There's something about the way my hand fits so perfectly in his. Something about the way his thumb moves along the back of my hand. It makes me feel like it's alright. Like everything is better than alright. Like it's supposed to be this way.

"I'm sorry," he whispers and plants a small kiss in my hair.

It's not a thought, not a conscious decision. I only pull my hand away from his so I can wrap my arms around him and bury my head into his chest.

"I'm sorry," I breathe into his chest and peek up at him. It's not our first fight or even the second. And each time it hurts more and more, but when he holds me again, when I know he still loves me, that feeling is the best in the world. I can't imagine anything feels better than that.

The door to Lydia's room opens, letting in the sounds of chatter outside the room and the construction noises from a set being built only twenty feet or so away. It's silenced when she closes it and she sags against the door with the biggest smile on her face.

The social butterfly that she is, she's been networking like crazy and I'm sure that she won't rest until everyone here knows exactly who Lydia Parker is.

"You have to leave this room, Harlow," Lydia says as she walks to the small fridge and grabs a bottle of water. "For real, there are so many people you need to meet." She takes a swig and then plays with the plastic cap between her fingers. "I don't know what's gotten into you, but this hideaway shit will not cut it here."

I take in her words and had I not seen Nathan, I'd take her advice in a minute. Shit, I'd be walking around right by her side this entire time, forcing the nerves down and doing what I need to in order to get my career on the right track. But the nerves reeling through me don't have a damn thing to do with work. It hasn't even been a blip on my radar since I saw him.

I fiddle with my phone and debate on how to tell her. It's eating me alive and I can't keep hiding.

"Who texted you?" she asks but doesn't wait for an answer before snatching the phone from my hand. It's the first time I've moved from her bed, hopping off but not bothering to reach out and take it. The defense is a natural one, but Lydia can take the damn phone if she wants.

"Are you mad that your mom is still being ... well, your mom?" she asks me after glancing at the text. Her voice holds nothing but concern and sympathy. My mother told me good luck, but added how worried she is. I'll be lucky if she lets me leave the house again when I go home after shooting wraps up. This isn't the life she had in mind for me and she's uncomfortable. But she won't hold me back. It's obvious she doesn't support my decision though.

I take the damn phone from her and lay back onto the bed.

"No, I knew she'd be like this." I don't blame my mom; it's just something she has to accept. She will. I have faith.

I cover my face with my hands. I don't have time for this stress and everything that's going on around me. It all needs to just stop. The memory of what happened that night keeps replaying in my mind. The sound keeps echoing in my head. It just won't stop. Nathan's a reminder of that night and I can't separate the two right now.

The bed dips as Lydia sits down next to me. "Look, I'm not going to sugarcoat this for you, Harlow." She puts both hands on her tanned knees and stares straight ahead before looking back at me. "This is fucking hard, but you need to get your ass out there and network. You need to be out there." She stresses each word, the savvy business side of her coming to the forefront.

"I, seriously, am not okay," I start to tell her, searching for the right words.

"Knock it off," Lydia says with a strength I wasn't expecting. "You are not going to give this up. Grab a hold of your big girl panties ..."

"I used to be with Nathan Hart," I interrupt her, spilling my secret and holding my breath as she stops midword and registers what I've told her.

Her words come out slowly as she says, "You ... used to date ... Nathan Hart."

Pulling my knees into my chest, I nod my head. It's so

much more than that though. We share a secret that was never told. A crime committed that was never given justice. And we're the guilty ones.

I can't speak. I can't start telling our tale. It was ten years ago and during high school. A short burst of puppy love maybe. But it's not the beginning that makes me hesitant to talk. It's how we ended and knowing I can never tell a soul what happened.

That night has never left me.

"Shut up!" Lydia squeals with a smile plastered on her face. She obviously can't read the thoughts going on in my head. She's oblivious to how nauseated I feel as she grips my arm and shakes me. "Tell me everything."

A moment passes in silence. I can't tell her shit. I've never told a soul, just like Nathan commanded.

I fell in love with a boy who broke my heart. That's about as simple as it gets and avoids the truth of the dark secret we share. It downplays my role and the guilt that will always stay with me.

I lick my lips as tears prick the back of my eyes and that's when Lydia seems to realize this isn't some childish retelling of a one-night stand.

"There's nothing to tell other than that ... we used to date back in high school and it ended horribly."

"That would be an interesting little tidbit to be leaked to the papers," Lydia arches a brow as she suggests the worst possible circumstances.

"No!" I'm quick to end that thought right where it begins and my immediate reaction has her raising her hands in defense. Fear is the overwhelming emotion. *No one can know.* "I don't want anyone to know."

He literally told me to forget his name. Every time I think about contacting him and just saying hello, I hear his words in my head. I don't want this getting out and him thinking I had anything to do with it. I can keep it polite, cordial, professional. Or at least that's the goal.

"No papers then. We'll keep this quiet?" she offers and I nod my head.

The idea of sneaking around on my tiptoes and avoiding him doesn't settle anything in me. I just can't stand to be around him, that's really what it is. I'll try to keep it professional and he'll destroy me by doing the same. But that's all there is between us. He made sure of that.

"I need to quit," I tell her and the last word cracks but I cover my face with my hands and pull myself together.

"First of all," Lydia starts as she runs her hand down my back in soothing strokes. "It's only four days that you have to be out there," she says and then adds with a shrug of her shoulders, "He may not even be here those four days."

I nod my head but I don't even know why. I don't know what I want. I'm supposed to take notes from Nancy after this, but I don't know how I'll be able to stay focused.

"Seriously though, you need to let it roll off your shoulders."

Her strength makes me look her in the eyes. "Don't let this keep you from what you really want."

What I really want is him. How stupid and naïve can I really be?

"Do you really think Nancy has something better for you right now?" Lydia asks me.

I don't respond; I can't even think of words. It's not the number of days or what's waiting for me in my career. It's simply the proximity to Nathan that makes me feel completely undone. Like my body can only move again once he tells me I can. Like I'm only breathing right now so I can live to see what he thinks of us meeting again. So unexpectedly, and so long since he's pushed me away.

"The pressure is on and Nancy isn't going to get another offer for you like this, let me tell you," Lydia starts and I know she's got a story up her sleeve, but I don't want to hear it.

"It'll be okay," I say out loud although I didn't mean to. We hid what we did back then, and we can hide it now.

"It will," Lydia says confidently and I can feel her eyes on me, but I can't look back at her.

"It'll kill me if he pretends he doesn't recognize me," I whisper and it's true. It's probably the worst thing he could do to me and it's exactly what I'm prepared for. It's what he did for the last two months of school, right up until he was arrested.

"If he does, he's an ass. And either way, you're going to kill it out there."

"Thank you," I tell her with every bit of sincerity. She shouldn't have to put up with me. I got used to being alone and I wish I was right now. With the exception of one person. *I'm pathetic.*

"I didn't get you this part so an ex could make you run away," she says and tries to smile, but my lack of humor or any trace of happiness keeps it away.

Ex isn't how I would describe him.

"Everything's going to be fine," Lydia tells me, breaking me away from my thoughts just as soon as the memories start to creep in. It's easy for her to say. She doesn't know a damn thing that happened.

Chapter 4

Nathan

Ten years ago
September 12

She's always running her fingers through her dirty blonde hair. The simple motion sends the sweet smell of lavender and something else my way. It's faint, but I know it's her. It's something sweet and soothing. If I think about her, or even if I see her across the lunchroom or in the school parking lot, I swear I can smell that scent.

I like sitting behind her in geography. I can watch the cute little things she does and it looks like I'm actually paying attention.

This is the only class I haven't gotten kicked out of so far. The stupid shit doesn't bother me as much when I can watch her. Even if she never looks at me twice.

The bell rings and the sound rips my eyes away from her and toward the classroom door as a few more students file through. Adam Waynes is the last in and his chair screeches across the floor as he crashes into his seat. He's loud as fuck and gets all the attention. At the thought, I look to her, to Harlow May. I'm expecting her to be watching the spectacle that would usually piss me off, but instead, those gorgeous blue eyes are on me. She's quick to look away, again her fingers flying to her hair and twirling her locks nervously as bright pink creeps into her cheeks.

She can be shy all she wants, but I caught her. I caught her looking. Even better, I made her blush. I did that.

It almost gives me enough courage to pull on her backpack straps as she walks in front of me to leave. I could give her bag a tug and force her to look back at me, but I don't. I stay behind like I have for the last few weeks and let her walk away.

But the next time she glances at me in geography, she doesn't avert her gaze when I look back.

And a few days later, she's the one tugging on my backpack.

I keep telling her I'm not good for her, but she doesn't listen though.

That's the very thing that will ruin us and we knew it from the start.

"Nathan!" Julie's shrill voice makes my brow furrow as I

raise my eyes to her. Her fingers are laced together as she folds her hands in her lap and lets out a huff of laughter. It's sweet, but nervous. "He does this sometimes," she tells Margo Hawkins, a reporter for some paper. I hate these things, but this one, I apparently couldn't get out of.

I force the hint of a smile on my face and readjust in my seat. I'm riddled with guilt, just like I've been every single day since I left her. But she was better off without me. I'm a different man now though.

"What's on your mind, Mr. Hart?" Margo asks.

Hally. Our past. Every moment I regret that led up to today.

"Nothing," I say and shake my head. Julie's smile slips and I see it from the corner of my eye. "I'm just so honored to be starring alongside Julie. She truly is a force to be reckoned with."

The smile comes back and this time it's genuine. I don't have a damn thing against Jules. She's a hard worker and obsessed with making the right moves for her brand, but right now I really could not give two shits.

All that's on my mind are the detailed papers Mark slipped under my door this morning. Everything about my Hally, who she's represented by and how she came to be here.

There's no way she knew I'd be here, but the coincidence is something I just can't drop. My Hally was sweet and innocent, but time changes everyone. I know this better than most.

"I have to ask," Margo says, leaning forward with a shy smile as she looks between the two of us. We're in the green room where these interviews are done and several men with recorders, cameras, and notepads are standing just behind Margo's chair taking in every word. I should force the charm and play the part. I know better than to let them see the real me. "Have you two had your first kiss on set yet?" Margo asks the ever-so-important question. It takes everything in me for me not to roll my eyes.

"Well, not yet, but I can tell you my husband is not looking forward to that one," Julie answers with a laugh and gives her patented smile. "There are a few days that he's choosing not to be on set," she adds with a flirtatiousness that makes Margo smile, but her humor is restrained as she looks to me for my response.

"Not yet," I answer as easily as I can.

Jules is nice and I've had plenty of heated moments with costars, some of which have gone too far and landed the "affairs" in headlines. More than a few times I knew that's all they were after when they sneaked into my dressing room.

The thought of Hally seeing other women come on to me makes me shift in my seat, the leather making the only noise in the small room as a man on my left jots something down in the notebook he's holding. Even if it's just for a scene and only for work.

"This role is different from your usual, Nathan. How are you preparing for it?" Margo asks me and I look past her to see several eyes on me, waiting for a response.

Clearing my throat, I struggle to even remember my role. When I started acting, I was the sidekick character with a smart mouth who got into fistfights. Not so far from the person I really was. The one who was always looking for trouble. Then the parts changed and I started playing deeper roles, ones where I was trying to do the right thing. More than once the characters I've played died fighting for what they believed in, right or wrong. The irony doesn't go unnoticed.

"Well, for one, I hardly cuss in this," I offer and smile, feeling the charm set in. Margo and Julie laugh and then I add, "Robby, my character in *Night Fire*, is definitely a different part in that he's from wealth and a formal upbringing, yet chose a life of crime, even if it is white collar."

The lines, scripts, and endless pages of my character's details come back to me. I nod my head and say, "It's definitely different and I'm enjoying it. I like the challenge."

The conversation moves seamlessly as I watch Julie and Margo go tit for tat in banter. I can barely stay focused. Mark's given me Hally's schedule and her first scene is tomorrow. She won't be able to hide from me then.

"And what are you most looking forward to, Mr. Hart?" Margo asks. "I know this must be tremendously different from cinema productions."

I'm mid-sentence when I see Hally. She's been on set for two days and hiding from me. Of course she'd show herself now when I'm doing my best to play my part and be the supportive costar.

Hally has a way of doing that to me. Throwing me off-kilter and bringing out a side of me that's raw with rough edges. I can't hide who I am from her; even worse, I don't want to.

My mouth's still open as I force my eyes back to Margo. No one seemed to notice that Hally stole my attention, even if it was just for a split second. No one but Julie.

I clear my throat and stare straight into Margo's eyes as if she were Hally as I say, "What I'm most looking forward to is getting to play a new character. To pretend to be someone else."

The second the last word leaves my lips, my gaze flickers to where Hally was standing, but she's no longer there. For a second, I almost think I imagined her.

"To forget who you are?" Margo asks me and I have to return my attention to her.

"That's what acting is, Miss Hawkins," I tell her, willing the image of Hally to come back, but she's long gone.

Chapter 5

Harlow

I'm just going to tell him, "Hi." Or maybe just look at him from afar. Either way, it's day three and I'm making progress. We both know we're tiptoeing around each other's existence. And there's no point to that.

The steam from the coffee billows into my face as I blow across the top. It's smooth and delicious as it goes down, but I hardly taste it. I keep my eyes straight ahead as I hide in the shadows just off set.

It's been ten years. Not long enough for the memories to fade, but hopefully long enough to be cordial.

I close the script in my hands as well, letting my finger run along the edge of the thick binding. *Night Fire.* That's the title it has for now, but that doesn't mean it's what the show will actually be called.

"Action," Stevens calls out from his chair and I can barely see him, the lights are so dim. The studio lights are high up, and all directed on the stage that's been set up to look like an office. An expensive one, at that. The floors are made to look like real wood when they're only linoleum, but the furniture is solid and expensive, most of it a deep rich brown. The little odds and ends, like the scattered papers and a mug on the desk, with paperbacks and awards on the bookshelf make it seem as though the office space is truly lived in. It gives personality to Robby's office.

Nathan's character is nothing like him at all. I avert my eyes and stare into the dark brown coffee. It needs more creamer. I swallow thickly and try to stop my train of thought.

I don't know who Nathan is anymore. It's possible I never really did know him.

The sound of the door shutting on set makes me focus again on the stage ahead of me. Nathan's eyes slowly lift, his fingers softly closing a book as he lets his eyes drift up and then back down to Julie, or I should say Miranda, Julie's character.

"Robby, are you hiding from me?" she asks coyly, walking across the set and my eyes instinctually move to the cameras that follow her, ever so smoothly.

She's a seductress and is damn good at it. The red dress she's wearing clings to her hips as she walks, and the same red color is painted on her lips.

"Robby, please," she purrs, leaning over the desk and giving him just a peek of her cleavage. I've watched her shows before and this role is different from anything else she's done. "We've known each other for how long?" she asks him, her perfectly shaped brow arching as she moves to sit on the edge of the desk.

This is a form of torture I think, watching Nathan and Julie act out this scene together.

I haven't watched a single one of his movies and I didn't ever intend to, but now I'm curious.

Nathan's expression is stiff, uncomfortable even. The papers rustle in my hands as I look down to read the scene again.

I flip the page over as quietly as I can and then peek up at Stevens, who looks pissed.

There's no way around it; Nathan's doing a shitty job. He isn't showing any interest in Miranda, Julie's character, in the least. Which is not what's written in the script at all.

"Cut!" Director Stevens yells out and it's the first time in days that I've heard his voice ring out with such frustration-laced authority. I've heard rumors about him, whispers in the industry about his interactions with actors being a bit hostile and demanding. It looks like I'm about to get a front row seat to exactly what they mean, but it makes me sick to my stomach, because I'm certain it'll be directed at Nathan.

The tension and disappointment in the air are palpable as the lights slowly get brighter and the onlookers, like me, begin to make faint noises while they shift their feet, flip through pages and whisper to their neighbors.

"You need to bring this scene to life. The emotion. There's passion between them." Director Stevens is calling out to Nathan and I watch as he nods his head repeatedly, but he doesn't stop looking at me.

My heart races and I can't breathe. *Stop looking, Nathan.* But it's not just his eyes anymore. The longer he stares at me, the more everyone else notices. I'm caught in their questioning stares and the only thing I can think is that I need to get out of here.

"Oh, that's why," I hear Julie say as she turns on her heels and walks back to the faux door. She flicks her hair over her shoulder and then looks back at me. My cheeks burn with embarrassment. "She shouldn't be here if she's distracting him."

I didn't do anything. I look everywhere except at her and Nathan, but all eyes are on me. Onlookers glance between Nathan and Julie, and then to me.

My breath is caught in my throat as I lower the papers in my hand. I wish I could run. All of this attention is solely because he won't stop staring.

I didn't make a noise. I didn't try to do a damn thing to distract him or anyone else. My teeth sink into my bottom lip and I keep my eyes on the ground, but I feel compelled to lift them. I can feel his dark eyes on me and when I raise them, sure enough, he's still focused on me. Not just a subdued look but a blatant stare that pierces through me, like a thin dagger meant to hold me perfectly still and threaten my very life.

The murmurs get louder and I know they're whispering about Nathan and me. Do they know something I don't?

"Stop it," I mouth to Nathan. It takes everything in me to do it. To even acknowledge that I can see him and he can see me. But he merely shakes his head slowly. Just once, but it's enough to let me know that he doesn't care about the awkward situation he's putting me in.

I try to turn away, ripping my eyes from Nathan's gaze, but it only leaves me caught in another. The director's. Stevens is staring straight at me and I only turn for a moment to see Nathan running his hands through his hair in frustration. He's no longer looking at me, and his back is turned, but that fact only makes the sickness churn more and more in my stomach.

"You." The loud voice is directed at me and it makes my body jump. Director Stevens points right at me, his voice bellowing in the confines of the set as he shouts, "Get off the set!"

Chapter 6

Nathan

Ten years ago
January 1

She can't make up her mind.

One day Hally loves me and I feel it. Down to the very core of who I am. And then I do something like say the wrong thing, and all of a sudden I don't appreciate her or whatever the hell she's prone to saying when she yells at me.

I don't know how to react or handle her. All it does is turn me on if I'm honest with myself. I hate the outcome though. It's easy for her to say things that hurt. Just as easy as it is for her to say the words that make me feel like I'm worth something to her.

She'll say she's sorry. She'll say she doesn't mean it.

She does all the talking, and that's the problem.

I sit in my car outside my house and think about the fight over and over. I know I could have just said I was sorry and I don't want to see her upset. That would have made her pause at least. That's my problem though, my dad made sure I learned not to speak up when I'm being yelled at.

The heat from outside is already leaking into the car, so I pull the keys out and make my way to 2204 Winston Street. I ignore everyone else as I get out of the car and walk inside. The steps are old, made of rough stone and uneven. I've fallen down them a few times as a kid, and they're the reason for the scar on my upper thigh.

I'm quiet when I walk in, listening to the sound of the TV playing in the living room. Taking a quick look in, I see Ma passed out in front of it. I don't know if she has night shift tonight or not, but I don't wake her up. I never do.

Not unless I want the shit beat out of me.

I thought Dad was bad until he split, but that's when Ma just took his place. Before I turn to go up the stairs, I see bottles lined up on the table in the kitchen. The pizza box from last night is there, open and empty, so at least I know she ate. Even though it looks like she had an entire case of beer along with it.

The old wooden stairs creak as I make my way up, two steps at a time. The higher I get, the hotter it gets, like stagnant heat.

I don't know why I even came home this early.

My bookbag smacks against the wall of my bedroom, right next to the nightstand. Along with my bed, they're the only furniture in the room. Even with the fan still going, it's hot as hell in my room.

If Hally hadn't snapped, I'd be with her. It's fucked up that I miss her; I know I can't keep her. Maybe one day if I come back to this town, like years from now, when I have a chance to do something with my life, we can be together again. Maybe then I could come get her and hold onto her.

But she'd still get pissed, and I still won't know how to say the right things.

I used to wonder if it was my fault that I didn't get along with my mother. I thought maybe it was the same as it was with Hally. That I just didn't know how to do the right thing. I tried though.

I swear I did. I thought maybe there was a silent truce between us, an unspoken love. My mother went through phases, with the drugs, the boyfriends. Whatever it was, I was quiet and stayed out of it, unless she needed me.

She kicked me out when I stopped her fuck-of-the-week boy toy from beating the shit out of her. He wasn't the first to smack her around. Just like Dad used to.

She didn't even give me clothes, nothing. Just kicked me out and then let him beat the shit out of me on the street. It was only days after what happened to Hally. It was my fault for reacting, I think. But I couldn't let him pull her hair and smack her around.

For months I tried to go back home; I didn't have a place to stay and just moved from one friend's house to the next, looking for a place to crash. I thought when he left, things would go back to what they were for me and my mom.

But I was eighteen, almost out of high school and therefore, not her problem anymore. Or so she told me.

Hally
Ten years ago
January 3

"Why aren't you eating?" Mom asks me again as I push the mashed potatoes around on my plate. My silverware clinks on the ceramic plate as I set it down.

"I'm just not hungry," I lie.

I can't stop thinking about the fight I got into with Nathan and whether or not he'll still love me tomorrow.

It wasn't supposed to turn into what it did. I wish Nathan would just care. I don't even know what we were fighting over. It doesn't matter. I hate talking to a wall. I hate it when he doesn't listen and the problem isn't fixed.

I can't just go on pretending like everything's okay.

My throat starts to close and I try to swallow, but I can't. I'm quick to reach for my glass of water and take a large gulp. I ignore my mother's eyes on me, assessing, worrying.

Maybe I should tell her. Maybe she would know what to do.

"Is something wrong?" my mom asks and my dad elbows her. The table is square, but my father sits at the spot that faces the front window in the dining room, so I still think of it as the head.

I eye the two of them as they share a glance.

"You can talk to me about anything, you know that," my mom says.

My dad keeps his eyes on the plate in front of him as he cuts up his pork chop and takes a bite. I've always appreciated how Dad lets me have time to myself. Mom's the opposite.

"I know," I tell my mom and scoop up a bit of the potatoes, but I just end up putting the fork down.

If Nathan didn't live where he does, I could just walk to his house. I don't have a car though, and he'd be pissed if I walked there to see him. And it's freezing outside. I did once, and it's the only fight we've gotten into where I was scared to talk back to him. He never yelled at me like that before.

It's because he loved me enough to want me safe. And that only makes me want to go to him even more.

I love him, more than anything and I wish we didn't fight. I don't know why we push each other like we do. We need it to stop, but I don't know how.

Tears prick my eyes and I push my chair back from the table.

"May I please be excused?" I ask, knowing I'm upsetting my mom by not talking to her.

"Baby," my mom says at the same time that Dad tells me to go ahead and leave.

The table shakes slightly as I get up and don't say another word, taking the escape Dad gave me.

I head straight to my room, wanting to sleep this night off until I can see Nathan tomorrow and try to make it right.

"Let her be. She's a teenager," I hear my dad say as I climb the stairs, holding on to the etched wood banister as I go.

My parents met when they were kids, but I don't think they'd understand. I don't even think they'd approve. So I don't tell them anything and maybe that was a mistake.

I never did tell my family that I'd fallen in love only to have my heart shredded in a way that was unimaginable. I think my mom knew though. She could always tell when something was wrong. Maybe that's why she hovered so much my senior year. Maybe it's why she wants me to stay close. I'm her baby and I always will be.

Some things I can't share with her though.

It's a story that's just meant for Nathan and me.

I wish I'd known how to talk to him back then. I wish I'd been smarter and known what he needed without relying on him to tell me.

Things could have turned out so much differently if we'd only known how to handle each other. But we came from different worlds and that was something we couldn't help.

Chapter 7

Nathan

My eyes look back at me from the mirror which is in the dead center of my dressing room. I haven't noticed how red they are; I haven't noticed the bags.

Three days of failed takes and threats of being pulled. Three days of Mark begging me to tell him what's wrong, so he can fix it before I'm fired.

Three days of me feeling like I'm eighteen again. Because I'm avoiding her. I'm a fucking coward for doing it, but I know she'll break me. She'll bring me back to the exact thing I've been running from.

It was so easy to just live when I didn't have a reminder of my past.

"You want to do something fun?" she'd asked me. She always asked me that. There was a sparkle in her eyes when she did it, too. Like she knew she'd get me into trouble. I can just see her whispering it off the set. I can see her luring me back to what we used to be and picture how she used to look at me. That desire in her eyes was the most addicting thing I've ever seen, ever felt. The taste of her lips and the feel of her curves as she moaned into my mouth is something I'll never have enough of. It'll be that question that pushes me to take my last breath.

September 17

"You want to do something fun?" she asks as she tucks her hair behind her ear. Her backpack shifts on her shoulder and she hitches it up as the bell rings again. The third and final bell.

Everyone's on their way out. The hallways are crowded and occasionally someone brushes against Harlow. She sways easily, seemingly not to notice. But I notice and it pisses me off. There's plenty of room to go around her. And I hate that they're distracting her in the least.

"What do you think?" she asks me and my gaze is drawn back to her.

Her eyes are the lightest shade of blue I think I've ever seen but there's a sparkle in them, and it reflects back at me as I stare at her. I let it last too, not saying a word and just letting her flirtatious suggestion hang in the air between us. It makes the tension grow and I live for that. For weeks she's been pushing me, asking little questions she already knows the answers to, just to say something to me.

She's playing with fire; she already knows that. But what she doesn't know is how damaging she'd be to me. The things I want to do to her and the depths I'd sink to in order to have her to myself. I'm no good for her, that's nothing new. But I want to make her mine and she can't know that. If she did, she'd be happy to let us burn together.

"*The bell rang,*" *I tell her just to say something and get my mind off her.*

"*I heard,*" *she says as I start walking to the exit. She follows me, refusing to take the hint.* "*So, let's go do something.*"

Everything in me is screaming at me to just tell her to go home.

"*I'm just going home,*" *I tell her and watch as disappointment temporarily dulls the brightness of her eyes. But she's not the type of girl to take no for an answer.*

"*Are you walking?*" *she asks.*

"*Yeah,*" *I tell her and shut my locker.*

She's quick to respond, "*I'll walk with you.*"

With that, I spin the combination on my lock and hang my bookbag over one shoulder. She looks up at me with those sweet eyes as she twists her hair around her finger like she's won. She knew I couldn't tell her no. She's my weakness.

"We can do whatever you want," she offers with a shrug that lifts her tank top up, exposing a bit of skin on her hip. She's quick to pull it down and cover herself back up and that alone is enough to make my fingers itch to touch her there.

"I think your idea of fun and mine are different, Harlow." She flinches at her name and I almost think I've fucked up somehow, but I know that's her name. I've whispered it over and over alone in bed.

She wrinkles her nose and says, "I don't like it when you do that."

"Do what?" I ask her.

"When you call me Harlow."

"It's your name, isn't it?"

"Yeah, but I don't know. It just sounds weird with you saying it," she answers me, continuing to follow me as I walk past two groups of kids that are clogging up the entrance to the school. I walk down three steps and although I felt her hold onto my backpack as I shifted through the people, I don't feel her anymore. I almost spin around to see if she's still with me, but the second I cave into temptation, I feel her soft hand brush against mine. It's like a spark of heat, a stroke of warmth and recognition flowing through me. I have to grip the straps at my shoulders to keep from taking her hand in mine.

My eyes narrow as I take in her words as the crowd slowly dissipates, walking toward the school buses lined up in rows. I don't get on mine and neither does she. She's so different. She's an odd girl, beautiful and naïve, but also alarmingly raw and genuine.

The sun's hotter than I thought it'd be; I'm already sweating, so I stop on the edge of the sidewalk that lines the asphalt road to the school to take off my t-shirt, displaying the plain white undershirt beneath. My eyes never leave her face though. I see how she looks at me and I love it.

"I saw you like playing cards," she says and tears her eyes away. Licking her lips, she starts walking again as I pick up my bookbag.

"Is that right?" I ask her. I bet she doesn't know shit about cards. I could teach her though.

"You were playing poker in free period." She's not in my free period. I give her a side-eye and it makes her blush. She's caught red-handed, but that doesn't make her miss a beat in her stride. My steps slow as we round Second Street. The turning point between my way home and hers.

"You gotta go home." I almost say her name, but I don't. I hate how it makes her flinch, but I do love the way it feels on my tongue.

"I can go where I want to," she bites back and looks up at me with a sharpness I didn't see coming.

I can tell her she doesn't belong down here, but she already knows.

I can tell her I don't want to walk with her, but that's a lie and I'm not sure she really gives a shit.

I can tell her I want her to come back to my room and I'll teach her how to play. But that's just taking advantage of the sweet little thing she is. Isn't it?

"You just won't quit, will you?" I ask her.

A trace of a smile plays at her lips and then she slowly shakes her head, making her backpack sway along with her dirty blonde hair. "Nope."

My head shakes in frustration as I look back down my street. The city's on a hill and the top, where we are now, isn't so bad. There's a nice park nearby and up the street are some pretty rich housing areas. But the closer you get to the bottom, to where the houses for the steel mill workers were first built, the houses aren't the nicest, to say the least. That's where I live. It's littered with five-and-dimes and liquor stores. And nothing else but where we live.

And I don't want her there.

The shame is something I didn't expect.

"Ha—Hally," I give her a nickname on the spot. "Let's go this way," I tell her and splay my hand on her lower back, sliding it under her bookbag. At first, she looks like she's going to protest, but she accepts it.

She likes my hand on her. She likes the nickname I gave her. She likes me.

There's no cure for the sickness she gave me that day by letting me lead her away from where I grew up. If she'd listened to me, who knows where we'd be now. But Hally doesn't listen and as much as she pushed me, I pushed her right back.

Knock! Knock! Knock! The obnoxious sound of repeated

banging on my door pulls me back into the present.

It pisses me off more than anything else.

The door opens quickly, hurriedly, but I stay still in my seat, grinding my teeth with frustration. I watch as Julie opens the door, allowing the sounds of the set to flood into the small room before closing it quickly behind her.

She doesn't wait for me to turn around. She doesn't wait for shit before saying, "Please tell me you aren't doing it on purpose?" It's not a question though.

"Hello to you too," I say as I turn in my seat to face her. I feel wound tightly, the memory begging me to come back to it.

"I'm doing my best to believe that you aren't completely sabotaging my role, but what happened today is complete horseshit, Hart."

A rough sigh leaves me as I run a hand through my hair and look at the mini fridge rather than at her. I already feel like shit, but the worst part is that I just can't bring myself to care about the production. It makes me a dick, but again, I just don't care.

"You're going to get fired--or worse, get me fired," she says and it irritates me. "Don't think I don't know that you were the first choice. Stevens has a hardon for you but I'm replaceable. I'm not naïve, Nathan. If you wanted a different costar all you had to do was say so, but now we're in production and it's known that I'm on this project."

"You're fine, Jules. No one's firing you," I tell her as I stand up to go to the door and let her out. I'm not interested in this shit.

"I swear to God if you fuck me, I will fuck you back ten times harder." It's hard to look at her with a straight face. She's angry, rightfully so. I'm not in the game, but none of this is about her and I don't have time for this shit.

"I have plenty of respect for you, Jules, and I can promise you I am not trying to ... fuck you." It's awkward even saying that to her.

"You need to get into the role," Jules says, her tone completely changed. "Whatever needs to happen," she says with a lack of conviction. "Whatever, just let me know how I can help you," she says and her eyes flicker to the floor and then back to mine.

"Nothing," I tell her before she's even finished speaking. "I'll get it right; I'm just not focused." I need to talk to Hally. I need to settle this thing between us. Whatever the hell it is.

"Do you need help ..." she starts in again, and I'm quick to shut it down.

"No."

"And what about that girl?"

My body tenses and I hesitate to answer, but say, "What girl?"

Julie's eyes roll as she puts her hands on her hips. "Don't give me that shit."

I let the anger simmer, not knowing what to say, but I settle on the truth. The bare truth. "She's just someone I used to know," I answer her.

She opens her mouth to give me her opinion or something, I don't know what, but I don't care to hear what she has to say. "I need to be alone right now," I say curtly. I'm basically telling her to get out.

The anger comes back in response to my cold return as she snaps, "Well get it together, Hart. I don't have time for this and I'm not going to be humiliated because you can't play a role."

The sound of the door slamming barely registers as I sit down on the bed and think about what I'm going to say to her.

The first question that comes to my mind is: *What is there left to say?*

And that answer is easy: *Everything.*

September 30

"Tell me what's wrong?" she keeps asking me over and over like she thinks I'm hiding something. If this is what being together entails, I'm good on my own. I don't have to tell her what a shitbag my mother's boyfriend is, or that we can't afford rent this month because he wiped out my mom's bank account. I don't have to, and I won't.

"I told you," I say as I slam the locker door shut and then face her. The wounded look in her eyes makes my anger wane. My words stay in the back of my throat, suffocating me as she visibly swallows.

"I just want to know," she tells me softly as her doe eyes gloss over.

I run a hand down my face and let out a sigh as I clench my fists and lean my forearms against the cold metal of the locker. I can almost see my reflection in it. Almost, but I can't. I can see hers though. The way she looks at me like she's hurt.

"Is it because I told my friends you're my boyfriend?" she asks me and then pushes the strap to her bookbag higher up on her shoulder.

If only it was that easy. The thought makes the corner of my lip twitch up into a smile as I turn back to her.

It's stupid. Holding her hand and putting a label on us. I don't get it. Anyone who looks at the two of us knows we're not going to work out. So why put a title on it? Why fuss over the details of something that isn't going to last?

"It's not that," I tell her simply and she looks back at me like she doesn't believe me. I'm on the verge of telling her. Of confessing. It'd be a relief to just tell someone, but not her. I don't want her to know.

"So, you're my boyfriend then?" she asks me, cocking a brow.

Fucking hell. I give in. "Sure," I tell her with a forced smile and she kicks me in the shin.

"Ow!" I mock yell at her and smile. "Yes, I'm your boyfriend," I say jokingly.

"Thank you, Nathan," Hally says sweetly, getting onto her tiptoes to wrap her arms around me. She does it so easily. Like she doesn't see everyone watching. And if she does, she doesn't

care. I keep my arms down, careful not to hug her back, but then it all changes. So suddenly, I almost don't realize what she's done.

She plants a soft kiss on my neck. It's wet, just a little, but it's the sound and the way that her hair brushes against my chin that make me wrap my arms around her waist. She does it again on my jawline. A small kiss and I find myself tilting my chin down and hoping for one on the lips, but she doesn't give it to me.

Instead, she rests flat on her feet and then smiles as her cheeks turn bright red. Before I can even utter a word, she grabs my hand and says, "Good. I can tell you need me to be your girlfriend." With a nod, she starts walking and I follow behind her.

That's the power she holds over me, but she wasn't prepared for the harsh reality of what being my girlfriend meant.

Neither of us were.

Chapter 8

Harlow

T*his is exactly what I needed*, I think as my shoes click against the floor to the dressing rooms by Stage Three. My body is on fire with anger. And embarrassment, but I push that aspect aside. The anger is so much easier to hold onto. It fuels me to keep walking with purposeful strides.

So many people turn to look at me as I storm up to his room, but I don't give a single one of them any attention. They don't know a damn thing other than the whispers going around the set.

Everyone saw the way Nathan looked at me, as if he was silently accusing me for his shitty acting. And they all heard what Julie said and the implications.

It is not my fault that Nathan isn't focused.

To top it off, Lydia let me know the "he said, she said" that's going around now: *Nathan told Julie you're a former flame and it's a problem you're here at all.*

I haven't had a soul even start a conversation with me before last night. Yet nearly a dozen people have come up to prod me about my relationship with Nathan. I get this anxious feeling in my gut every time ... like he's talking shit about me or trying to get me fired.

And I'm not going to stand for this.

My knuckles are white by the time I raise my hand to his door, but before I can get any satisfaction out by pounding my fist against it, the door swings open.

At first, Nathan's surprised, simply because someone happened to be right there when he opened the door. I'm a bit taken aback as well. But then recognition dawns on him and his eyes narrow. I don't give him a chance to turn me away. I walk right in, brushing against his hard, hot body, ignoring how the heat races through me from just that little touch. My hair sways against my shoulders as I turn around to face him. I'm rocking back and forth from foot to foot slightly as the urge to fight wanes little by little.

I hold on to the fire, clenching my teeth, and focusing on exactly how I was going to start.

His motions are slow, deliberately so. He takes his time closing the door, even taking a moment to glance out and see who's watching. My self-consciousness gets the best of me for only a second. Maybe a split second. Until the door closes, leaving us alone and I remember exactly what happened.

"What's going on?" I ask him evenly, although I'm sure he can tell I'm pissed. "You can ignore me all you want, but fucking up your takes and blaming it on me is not okay." My throat feels hoarse as I finally get the words out.

His brow rises slightly and he cracks his neck to the left, seemingly unaffected. Bastard.

"I didn't come to the set to disturb you or," I raise my hands in the air dramatically, "or throw you off your game."

He's quiet. He's always done this to me. He leaves me to be the one to carry the conversation. He likes to see me squirm, but I'm not willing to play his game right now.

"I didn't even know you'd seen me!" I screech and the rawness of my voice hurts my throat as the words escape.

Nathan stands there, so much taller than me, muscular and brooding in a way that should intimidate me. Maybe even threaten me, but all it does is make me angry.

He wanted to hurt me.

My teeth grind against one another as I take two steps forward and shove my palms against him. His muscles are firm and unmoving; the shove doesn't make his hard body move in the least. But it provokes him. It accomplishes exactly what I knew it would.

"What are you doing here?" he asks, looking down at me

as his body sways with the need to move. His feet are solidly planted though. He's only giving me the tiniest bit. And it hurts.

"I didn't know you'd be here," I say and my throat closes. My fight is practically gone.

I loved him. He's the first man I loved. My first in every way.

"I find it hard to believe," he says.

"Fuck you," I spit at him and take half a step back. "If I wanted to see you ..." I start to say, but he interrupts me.

"You'd have come days ago. I know." His eyes heat and his expression morphs from disinterest to pissed off. "Yet you didn't, and now you're here. Why is that?"

He's angry I didn't come see him? He's got to be kidding me.

"You knew I was here. Didn't you?"

His eyes flash, and he tries to play it off but I saw.

"This isn't on me. This is on you," I say and push my pointer finger into his chest. "You're the one who ended it and said to stay away." *You're the one who left me when I needed you.* The memory comes back and I practically choke on the words. "This is on you," I repeat and try to make the words come out strong, but I've never sounded so weak in my life. I'm back to being the frightened girl I was that night. Left alone and abandoned and with no one to help me.

I hate what he does to me. I hate how much I crave it too. He's silent and that's what makes me shove him again.

It destroys his last bit of restraint.

"Is this what you wanted, *Harlow*?" he says as he lowers his head and closes the space between us, grabbing my hips and pushing me backward. If I wanted to, I could let him do it. I could let him push me onto the bed. But I don't. I smack his hands away, my heart racing wildly. Yes, it's what I want. But he'll never know that. I won't let him know what he does to me.

"Why are you such a dick?" I sneer at him. "I didn't do shit to you," I tell him as tears prick my eyes. I won't cry though, I never do. I just bury things deep down, right where the memories of us belong.

His brows raise in feigned shock. "Me?" he asks, pointing to his chest. "What the hell did I do to deserve that, Harlow?"

It shouldn't get to me like it does. I pictured this happening in so many ways. I didn't think he'd still hate me though. I thought maybe time would ease some of the tension, but it's so raw and right in front of us. It won't be ignored.

"You told me to stay away and I did," I tell him.

"But now you're back."

"Some would say you're back."

"So, now I need to stay away from the entire East Coast?" he says sarcastically, decreasing the space between us by taking another large step. It's not lost on me that I'm nearly backed into a corner. And that's exactly how I feel.

All because of one night that I so desperately wish I could take back.

"It's been ten years, Nathan." There's a softness in my voice I didn't intend to have. "I wish I could change the past.

Even if you hate me, could you just ..."

I can't finish, although I want to. I want to plead with him and try to get on some neutral ground. But he beats me to it and silences me in a way I can't refuse.

He crashes his lips against mine and it's more than I can bear. My body goes weak, each nerve ending on fire and acutely aware of the heat of his body. His hands travel down to my waist, his blunt fingernails scraping against my skin and making my back arch.

I'm breathless when he pulls away, a flurry of emotions consuming me and taking me back to when I was his and he could make everything better.

"Hally," he whispers in the space between our lips, his hot breath overwhelming me, leaving my head spinning with nothing but want and gratitude. My fingernails run up his shirt along his back, up to his broad shoulders. It's like I'm home. His warmth, his touch, the reverence when he says my name.

I hold onto him with everything I have, holding him close to me like I wanted to do that night. And he does the same. Soothing me and cradling my body against his.

This is crazy. *We're* crazy. I guess some things don't change.

"You shouldn't be here," he whispers as he lowers his lips to the crook of my neck and nips me in admonishment. The action is directly linked to my clit, making it throb with need.

He pulls back slowly, both of us catching our breath, and he stares into my eyes. I lean into his touch as he brushes the hair away from my face to cup my cheek. "You aren't supposed to be here."

My heart stutters in my chest. Skipping its rhythm as it tries to figure out how it's supposed to beat. I search his eyes for something. For the anger that pushed me away. For forgiveness, which I'm so desperate to have. But all I see is desire. And that's something I can hold onto. I can be consumed by it. I was before. Blindingly so.

"It was an accident," I tell him. He licks his lower lip and my eyes are drawn there before I meet his eyes again. "But I think it happened for a reason."

"We should talk," I say as though it's a suggestion, but really, it's a question. One I desperately need him to answer. So many unspoken things still remain between us. They eat away at me, drowning me in an abyss of unknown. And fear. I had to live with it all on my own. I don't want to anymore; I never wanted to.

"Not right now. Not yet," he answers me and looks back with pleading eyes. He's the one with all the power and both of us know he doesn't need my permission, but he craves it. And like a moth to a flame, I'm addicted to giving it to him.

Chapter 9

Nathan

She's a mistake. A sweet mistake I can't say no to.

Years and years of telling women no, letting them down gently or being blunt when I had to. Yet she walks in, and I can't turn her away.

It's got to be the guilt, or our past together. Both are synonymous.

How can you look into the eyes of the love of your life, and tell her to fuck off?

"Let's take it from the top," Stevens yells out and instinctively my feet rock, preparing for the scene, but this one's not for me. I crack my neck and let out a tense sigh as I cross my arms and stare at the set from off the stage.

Hally's gorgeous in that getup. It's just black leggings and a cream silk blouse. Simple, but utterly gorgeous.

She's a friend of Miranda's in the scene and an instigator. It's the same set from my last scene. The one I failed miserably to put into action.

"Spread the papers out when you go looking for a file," Stevens yells down from his high chair to the right of me. He's only a few feet away from me, but even I have a hard time hearing him. He refuses to use a bullhorn, but Hally nods diligently, ready to do her part. I love the way her mouth parts open and she licks her lips as she prepares herself.

I can see her bending over the desk just like Julie was doing yesterday. Even in that blouse, without an inch of cleavage showing, I could slip my finger down the center and pop the buttons open one by one. She'd crawl on top, well she would try to, but I ...

"Action!" Stevens yells out, distracting me from my thoughts. A low grunt of frustration leaves me as I shift from side to side, ignoring the growing erection in my pants.

"Where is it?" Hally mumbles under her breath and I already know Stevens is going to call out and interrupt her.

"Louder. Start from the top!" he yells.

I don't like the tension that runs through me as Hally stops only seconds after starting and heads back to the door. She stands just inside, her hand on the knob and waits for him to call out action for her to shut it as though she's just entered and walk quickly to the other side.

"Take two. Action!"

She may be new and the subtleties hard to grasp, but the way she looks back over her shoulder as if she's checking to make sure no one followed her and how light she is on her feet so her heels don't make much noise, are tells she's really into the part. She's going to do damn well, I can feel it.

She chews on her bottom lip as she runs her fingers over the edge of the desk and tries to open the drawers. It's nearly soap opera material, but the scene itself calls for that. The sound of the drawers, locked and unwilling to give her access is the only sound I can hear. There are at least a dozen.

"I want you to play Miranda's part; Nate, get on set." Stevens isn't light with his words. He's demanding and I know I can't go against what he's suggesting. I clear my throat and stride to the chair at the desk, avoiding looking at everyone else who's watching. There's not as large a crowd as there usually is.

"Miranda's?" Hally's voice is quiet, disbelieving and unsure.

"You know her part, don't you?" Stevens asks.

"Yes, yes, I know it," Hally answers him but she doesn't look up. She's nervous as fuck and I know she has to be feeling less than confident. If Julie were here, she'd have a fit that anyone else was playing her part, especially given the circumstances.

"Makeup?" one of the production assistants asks, but

Stevens waves her away.

"It's just to see something," he answers her and I close my eyes as I grip the arms of the chair.

"Can I have a minute?" Hally asks hesitantly.

I answer at the same time as Stevens, "No."

I don't bother to look at him or anyone else. Only at Hally.

"You need to be closer," I tell her. "Start here," I pat the edge of the desk, right where she's supposed to stand before trying to tempt me. I already know what's on Stevens' mind and he's right. His instinct is correct.

Hally swallows thickly and lets out an unsteady breath as she shakes out her hands.

"It's alright, Hally," I whisper and give her a smile that's just for her. "All you have to do is not take no for an answer."

She smiles back at me, this sweet tempting look. Her blue eyes shine clear and brightly back at me. Like it's a game. She likes games and high stakes. She always has. "Push me, Hally," I whisper and it's then that the murmurs get louder.

"Quiet on set!" Stevens yells and then immediately calls out, "Action!"

"Robby," Hally says in a sultry voice I've never heard from her. She tucks her hair behind her ear, but not in the usual way. It's slower, meant to be seductive and the soft brush of her fingers against her blouse as she reaches down to lean against the desk draws my eyes right to her breasts. "Have you been hiding from me?" she asks me and then slowly the corners of her lips curl, but she stifles the smirk by biting on her lip.

"Maybe," I answer her and then second-guess myself and wonder if that was really my line or not.

She straightens her back, slipping her ass onto the desk and then leans toward me, enough so that my fingers itch to do exactly what I was thinking about moments ago. "How long have we known each other?" she asks me and I slip in and out of the truth.

"It feels like forever." The words fall from my lips naturally.

She tilts her head and lets her fingers walk across the table, skipping over the papers, her eyes focusing on them, but I can't take my eyes from her. I'm wondering what she's doing, what she's thinking. Wondering if she likes this.

"I think I need a favor from my dear old friend," she purrs and then licks her lips and looks up at me, placing her palm on the edge of the desk closer to me and leaning forward.

I can't think of my lines, what I'm supposed to say. But I know I'm supposed to fuck her on this desk. Miranda takes Robby for a damn fool. And that's exactly what I am for Hally. A damn fool.

I lift my head slowly, not quickly like I did last night. It was instinct then, but right now it's a choice. My hand moves to her throat, but I simply let the backs of my fingers stroke lightly along her skin. The corners of my lips curve into a smile as a shiver runs down her body.

I have to hold back how much it turns me on when she shyly peeks up at the director, falling out of character and feeling self-conscious at how easily I'm playing her body.

I move my pointer finger up her throat to her chin, grabbing her attention and forcing those baby blues back onto me.

"I've been right here the whole time, sweetheart," I say and brush the rough pad of my thumb along her lower lip. "Just tell me what you need and I'll make sure you get it."

Her shoulders rise and fall steadily as she looks back at me with those big doe eyes. Like she's caught in a trance, or worse, needing to decide on which way to go. Play along with me, kiss me and keep pretending. Or break away and leave.

Kiss me. Please, Hally, give me what I need.

As if she read my mind, her hands fly to the side of my head and she crashes her soft lips against mine. I don't waste a second, pulling her body across the desk, letting the papers scatter onto the floor; something else drops with them, causing a loud crash but I don't bother to see what it was. Her body is so hot and soft, I slip one hand under her blouse and the other around her small waist, pulling her toward me and like the good girl she is, she spreads her legs for me.

I only break our kiss as I stand up, shoving her chest down so she's pinned to the desk, her legs spread as she catches her breath and waits for me over her.

I reach up to loosen the tie that's supposed to be in place.

But I'm not dressed for this shoot and the moment I realize it, Stevens yells out, "Cut!"

Hally's quick to sit up, to scramble off the desk, tugging her blouse down and brushing her lips with the back of her hand. I stare at her and she stares at the back wall of the set.

"Brilliant!" Stevens yells. "We have a new Miranda."

Chapter 10

Harlow

Page Six of the New York Post

Heartthrob and former bad boy, Nathan Hart, is at it again. He's making headlines, but for all the wrong reasons.

Born and raised in New York, Nathan hasn't set foot on the East Coast since he left it nearly a decade ago, shortly after he was released from incarceration at only nineteen years old. He caught his biggest break being cast as the bad boy lead in the blockbuster hit, Cold Metal. He then had hit after hit portraying tortured souls on the big screen in LA, but back in NYC, he's making his television debut on Night Fire.

Costarring with Julie Rays, it was rumored to be the biggest *television hit this year.*

But an altercation sent sparks flying amongst the entire cast. All because of a blast from his past, newbie actress, Harlow May. She's made waves on the set, but not in the way you think.

Nathan is off his game and unable to do his job, according to costar Julie. Yet she's the one who's been demoted and the production is inundated with the sexual tension between Nathan and Miss May, the new star of the show.

Nathan's declined to comment, but Harlow seems anxious to spill the beans on everything that happened between them so many years ago.

With an expunged criminal record from his youth and everything at stake, Mr. Hart may be playing with more fire than he can handle.

The steam from the shower floods into the main area of the dressing room as I open the bathroom door. I'm quick to shut it before it heats up the entire room. It's Julie's dressing room. Well, it used to be. She's fired and now I'm her replacement.

I'm tired more than anything, although I feel a little sick over it all. This is a mess and a half and I don't know what I've gotten myself into. I just know it's drama all the way around and I didn't sign up for this.

But there isn't a shot in hell that I'm going to leave.

September 24

I'm not leaving this car until he kisses me.

I refuse to be the first, but I also refuse to wait any longer.

Four days of flirting with him are enough for him to know that he can kiss me. My heart clenches at the thought that he doesn't want to, which is a very real possibility.

"Alright," he says, scratching the back of his head as we sit in front of my house in his old Honda Civic. He turns the volume to the music down and then puts a hand on the shifter. "I'll see you tomorrow," he says easily. I get the feeling that he's waiting for this to end and I can't let that happen. I know deep down inside of me that there's something meant to be between us.

I nod my head, putting my hand on the handle and wishing I didn't feel this way. I wish I had more confidence, but I don't. I'm the one who's chasing him, that should tell me enough, shouldn't it? I'm stupid. So stupid.

The realization springs me forward. I should have known better.

"Hey," Nathan says as I pull on the lever and put one foot on the asphalt below. His heavy hand lands on my thigh and I sit back stiffly in my seat to face him again, praying my true feelings don't show.

Judging by his expression, they show.

"What's wrong?" he asks.

"I just wish you wanted me as much as I want you," I tell him, knowing full well I'm exposing more of myself to him than I want to; more than I've shown anyone else.

"Harlow, you don't really want me," he says like this is a joke. It pisses me off.

"First of all, don't tell me what I want, and second of all, that's not my name."

His brow furrows with both confusion and anger as he replies, "Everyone calls you Harlow and you don't snap at them."

"You're not everyone," I admit to him, leaning forward as tears sting in my eyes. I feel stupid as my body gets hotter and hotter sitting here. I should just blame it on my hormones.

"Hey," he says and draws my attention back to him as he licks his lips. "I want you, okay?" he says softly and then stares at me for a long moment.

He moves slowly as he leans forward and puts his hand on my chin.

This is it! My heart feels like it'll burst, but at the same time I feel nervous, like it has to be perfect.

His thumb brushes along my cheek and then he leans in that much closer until he brushes the tip of his nose against mine. I close my eyes and tilt my chin up, just enough to give him the permission he's looking for.

I'll never forget how it feels to have his hot lips against mine. It's not just my lips, it's my entire body that reacts. My blood flows with a heated desire. My fingers dig into the cushion of the seat. My toes curl in my shoes.

It's over too soon and I try to protest, reaching up to grab his hand as he pulls away. But when I open my eyes, his are still closed, for the longest moment. And I savor the sight.

"Trust me, Hally," he says with his eyes still closed, "I want you."

I let out an easy sigh at the memory, my chest filled with warmth. So many memories are coming back to me. Each of them another reason to run back into his arms.

Just as I slip my fingers to the end of the towel that's wrapped around my body, ready to strip it off, the door opens and I nearly have a heart attack. I grip the towel tighter as the door opens and then closes just as quickly, leaving Lydia standing in the room with a huge ass grin on her prettied-up face.

How the hell does she always look so bright eyed and happy? She barely sleeps, yet there's not even a trace of bags under her eyes. And with her hair pulled back in a tight ponytail, she looks peppy and ready to take on the world.

"That was a-fucking-mazing," she says with enthusiasm that forces a smile to my lips.

I'm still taking it all in, but I smile back and tell her, "Thanks." I chew on my lip wanting to say more, but I can't think of what to tell her. It feels like I'm holding everything back. I suppose I am, but for good reason.

Lydia doesn't seem to notice. If she does, she doesn't let on.

She grabs a bottle from the fridge and sits on the far side of the bed and lets her heels rest on the edge, wrapping her arms around her knees. "Julie quit," Lydia says quietly and then takes a swig from the bottle of water. "Did you hear?" she asks me.

A grimace hovers on my lips as I pick up the lotion from the vanity. My skin's still damp from the shower. "About Julie?" I ask her and pop the bottle open. The soft smell of lavender floats toward me as I let a line of lotion trail down my right leg and then rub it in.

"Yeah, I heard," I tell her and then swallow the lump in my throat. Julie didn't have the nicest things to say about me. But I have to keep in mind that she doesn't know me and she's obviously upset. I had to tell myself that over and over in the shower.

If she hates me, it's not because of me, really. It's just the situation.

"Don't worry, she's gonna get over it," Lydia says between sips of water and then tightens her ponytail.

I massage the lotion into my other leg as I think about how Julie had to be told that a nobody was taking her part. If I was her, I'd be pissed.

"I think she started the rumor about you and Nate anyway."

It's weird that everyone calls him Nate. My nose scrunches at the thought of calling him that.

"Did she really?" I ask her and she shrugs. My brow's pinched at the thought of Julie starting rumors. But then again, I don't know her either.

"Probably," she answers and then tosses the empty bottle into the small bin right next to the fridge. "She saw the way he looked at you," she adds as she opens the fridge for another. "You want a drink?" she asks me, looking over her shoulder.

I shake my head no. A frown forces its way onto my face until my lips are puckered, while I rub the remainder of the lotion into my hands and ignore the fact that Julie may have started a rumor that Nathan and I used to date. It's true, so it doesn't matter much really.

"You didn't tell anyone, did you?" I ask Lydia as the thought occurs to me. Her brow furrows as she shakes her head. Her long black hair sways back and forth with the forceful motion. "Not a soul," she answers.

My clothes are on the seat of the chair. Just a pair of black leggings and a baggy t-shirt with, "Coffee first!" printed on the front in a swirly font. Lydia takes the hint before I even have to tell her and she falls onto the small bed and stares at the ceiling as I get dressed.

"So, are you two," Lydia hesitates to finish, but she does, "like, back together?"

It's quiet for a moment as I take in the knowledge that rumors are going around, and to be very honest with myself, I don't even know what to make of Nathan and me. I'm drowning in my emotions and waiting for him to make the next move. Maybe that's a mistake.

"I don't know what we are," I tell her as I bend over and towel dry my hair before wrapping it up and sitting it on my head. The large motions cue her to look back at me and she cracks up laughing.

"You look too ridiculous with that thing on your head to be talking like that." I can't find it in me to laugh with her. I want to. I don't want to feel this anxiety and uncertainty. I've only ever had that in my life with Nathan. *Only him.*

"Seriously, it can't be that bad," Lydia says as she appears to tune into my mood. "You guys got into a fight and broke up on bad terms."

I shrug and then take a seat at the vanity. I want to unload everything. It's like a weight on my chest that won't get the hell off.

"Did he cheat on you?" she asks.

"No," I answer as I put my elbow on the edge of the chair and then my chin in my palm.

"Did he hurt you?" she asks and I'm quiet. I almost say no out of instinct, but he did. He made me feel like it was all my fault. Like I couldn't talk to anyone about it. I swallow the lump growing in my throat and let out the breath I've been holding.

"Not physically." I stare at the ceiling and wait for her to say something, but I'm greeted with silence.

I lower my head, balancing the stupid towel and then finally reach up to just take it down, running my hands through my damp hair.

"What did he do?" Lydia asks with a crestfallen expression.

"He tried to save me," I tell her, remembering that night and how he was my knight in shining armor. But knights come in times of war and their armor doesn't survive without scratches, or dents. Without blood.

Lydia sits up on the bed with a deep sigh. She hunches forward with her elbows on her knees and her hands on her forehead before looking back at me. "I don't know if you're being melodramatic or if something insane happened. I'm lost here, Harlow."

"He did the right thing. It's just that the right thing wasn't good, and it made us ..." I can't finish. It tore us apart. It made us see how foolish we were. It showed how stupid I was and how destructive we were together.

"But that was back then," Lydia says. "Ten years ago," she adds, raising her voice.

I understand how ridiculous it is. "Yeah, I just haven't seen him since."

"Well, can you put it behind you?" she asks as I stare at the thin carpet on the floor.

"I think he'd like to pretend it never happened," I tell her honestly. I can't explain why it hurts my chest so badly to think about just erasing that night.

"And you?" she asks in a voice with such compassion I have to raise my gaze to hers.

"I would do anything to take it back."

Chapter 11

Nathan

St. Gerard is a massive skyscraper, equipped with its own restaurants, office buildings, and five-diamond rooms; they call it a hotel, but it's practically a resort. You could get lost in here if you wanted to. You could live a happy life and never even step foot outside this building. You could also avoid someone else living here for as long as you had to.

If that's what you wanted to do. Judging by the fact that I'm obsessed with knowing Hally's room is in the east hall of the fourteenth floor, that's not what I intend to do. Room 14206. There's no name on the door, but Mark assures me she's here. She'd better be.

I haven't seen her in days. She's avoiding me again and it

kills me. She doesn't have a choice, and neither do I.

I clear my throat as I walk past a small crowd of people by a cart set up for bagels and coffee. The rich scent fills my lungs as I walk by, ignoring how a few of the people creep forward, one with her hand out as if she'd like to stop me.

I pretend I don't see her or her attempt to initiate a conversation, keeping my strides even and fairly quick. There are no verbal objections and I guess I'm grateful for that.

A single kiss, and I feel like I'm coming undone. A manufactured one at that. But it *felt* real. The electricity and tension between us were all too real on my part. If I still know her, if she's the same girl she was ten years ago, it's the same for her.

With each step of my sneakers sinking into the luxurious carpet of the fourteenth floor, I know I'm getting closer and closer to doing something stupid.

I don't give a fuck. I want her. I need to have her again. At all costs. But I need to play this right. Hally's always been emotional and hard to predict, like wildfire, and I don't know what it is I do to her that sets her off.

I'll be careful though, since I know better now. Which is damn good since I'm standing in front of her door.

My knuckles rap against the door three times. They sound even and controlled, unlike my beating heart.

As I shove my hand into my pocket, the door swings open. Hally's unknowing at first, with a curious look on her face and then it falls. She stands in the doorway, her grip tightening on the door.

"May I come in?" I ask her with feigned politeness. I'm conscious of the fact that people are watching; they're always watching, which is why we need to talk. Or at least it makes a damn good excuse for me to insist we talk.

Hally doesn't answer. She simply breathes out slowly, like it hurts her to let it go and then steps to the side, opening the door wider. Her eyes stay on me, but they're wide and swirling with a mix of emotions.

She's scared. I've seen this look before, so many times back in high school. It's the look she always had before we'd get back together. When she'd hide from me, run away, or push me away, but she'd always come back with that look in her eyes. Her mouth shut as she'd wait for me to tell her I was sorry, or that I forgave her, or simply that I wanted her back.

My blood courses with heat and excitement and so much more. She's putty to me at this moment, waiting for me to make the decision. It was always so easy to go after her again, and it's just the same now.

With every step I take inside, Hally takes a step back until her knees hit the bed. "Hally," I say her name as I turn around slightly and gently push the door so it's partially closed, just enough for privacy, but not enough to make anyone question what's going on inside her dressing room.

"Nathan," Hally whispers my name and it comes out

ragged but filled with desire.

"I think we should talk," I say evenly and then run my hand through my hair. "Can I sit?" I ask her, again just to be polite and cordial, but also to keep her on her toes, to mess with her and prolong this tension. I love it when she's like this.

Maybe that's why it was so easy to push her. The make-up sex and seeing just how much she wanted me was something I could never resist. Maybe it's a vice of mine, fighting with Hally just to get closer to her. Everyone wants to be desired.

She nods her head, swallowing thickly and then glancing at the door before sitting on the edge of the bed. "Nathan, I want you to know," she starts to speak before I can sit and it's unexpected.

She sucks in a breath and then clears her throat before looking up at me. "I understand that I'm invading your territory a bit," she says her words carefully, squaring her shoulders and being as professional as possible. The confidence and even arrogance that I had when she first opened the door threatens to leave me, but I hold on to the way she felt as she squirmed underneath me on set. She wants me, I know that much and it's all I need. She can pretend this is something else if she wants to. It wouldn't be the first time.

I grip the top of the chair at the vanity as I take a seat, giving her the floor to get whatever it is that's on her mind off her chest.

"I was going to come see you sooner. I just ..."

"Couldn't find me?" I ask her sarcastically.

"I didn't search you out or even know you were here when I was asked if I wanted the part. I didn't do this on purpose, I promise you."

"You couldn't have; no one knew I'd signed on," I tell her to let her know I believe her and ease the strained tension.

"I'm not here to threaten you or say anything at all, or bring up anything that happened," she says and every word seems to come out faster, rushed and stealing her breath. It makes my blood run cold. If Hally wanted to hurt me, she could have long ago. If she wanted to threaten me or hold something over my head, or even blackmail me, she would have already.

I never thought she would, but I have to admit more than a few times, the thought came to mind. It was fleeting, but it was there. Part of me even wanted it.

"You're a really good actress," I tell her, my voice low in my throat. She questions the intention of my words. As if I'm questioning the authenticity of what she's saying. Making her defensive and on edge as she licks her lips and crosses her arms.

I shouldn't push her like this. I shouldn't instigate a fight. I know that I shouldn't, but the thought of her pushing me right back is making me hard as steel.

"Thank you," Hally responds, although her words hold an edge to them and her eyes narrow slightly. She purses her lips and then her tongue slips out, wetting her bottom lip and forcing me to remember how she tasted, how good it felt to kiss her again.

I sit back in my seat and tilt my head as I speak to her, ignoring her confession and the tension regarding our past. "I mean it." I rest my elbow on the vanity and place my chin in my hand. "I wasn't expecting you to fall into the role so easily."

She huffs the smallest of laughs, but it's genuine and it brings a lightness to the air and a blush to her cheeks. She shrugs off the compliment, so like herself, but I know it affected her just by the relaxed position she takes when her eyes finally reach mine again. Her movements are slow as she leans back on the bed, the soft creaking filling the room.

"You're not so bad yourself," she says easily and flirtatiously.

A noise from behind me forces me to turn around. I left the damn door open, mostly for Hally's sake but also to keep me from being stupid. Although that's exactly what this is.

Nancy Welsh knocks on the open door, peeking in hesitantly as she does. I'd recognize her anywhere with her salt and pepper hair that looks like she dyed it to be that way. She's well known in the industry and has a solid reputation. She looks into the room, glancing between the two of us from behind her thin-framed glasses. "I just wanted a word if you have the time?" she asks Hally.

"Of course," Hally answers and practically jumps from the bed. Her hands are folded in front of her as though she's a child who's been caught with her hand in the cookie jar.

Half of me is pissed by it, but the other half of me loves it and begs me to make myself even more comfortable in her room.

"Actually, I think tomorrow would be better?" Nancy says and looks pointedly at me. Hally isn't catching on in the least. Her brow furrows and she shakes her head.

"Now is fine," she says and a rough chuckle vibrates up my chest, catching the attention of both women.

I clear my throat and slide my hands across my worn jeans as I lean forward and ask Nancy, "Could I just have a few minutes?"

She gives me a tight smile and looks back at Hally, waiting for her to catch on, but she doesn't. Hally never was the best at reading the subtle intentions of others, which is ironic, considering how well she's able to portray them herself. "You can have all night," she says easily and then waves goodbye, ignoring the gasp of a plea from Hally.

Nancy closes the door behind her and leaves the two of us alone, with Hally left standing awkwardly and staring at the closed door.

"She thinks we're going to fuck," I tell her.

That gets her eyes on me with her mouth opened in disbelief. "She knows I'm not like that," Hally answers and I never would have thought those words could make me so hard.

"Not like what?" I ask her, although I already know. Mark provided me with a list of her former boy toys. It's a short list and I'm grateful for that. More importantly, she's currently single and "too busy working her ass off" to date.

Which is just perfect for me.

Hally waves off my question, retaking her seat and looking at me and then the closed door before asking, "Are we okay?"

Her face is etched with genuine concern. I hate it.

"Yeah, we're okay," I tell her, crossing my arms and leaning back. She's wounded and scared and I'd bet anything she'd fall into my arms if I let her. And I want her so badly, but maybe I shouldn't. A small voice whispers to let her be. That I don't have to do this.

But I ignore that bastard voice and clear my throat to ask her, "Do you want to practice some lines together?"

She sees right through me, although she does glance at the stack of papers on her vanity. Her script. It's fresh and neat. Obviously an updated version since her role has changed.

"It must be difficult changing roles during filming," I say as if I'm genuinely interested in helping her.

"I'll be fine, I promise," she says and that look comes back to her eyes. She's waiting for me to offer more. Hopeful for it, even if she's scared.

"We don't need to practice lines then," I tell her, holding her gaze and watching it heat.

"You want to ... talk?" she asks.

"Not really," I answer her honestly and she immediately looks away, brushing her hair from her face. Maybe I shouldn't have said that. It's been too long to just assume she'd come back to me so easily. "We could just catch up," I offer her, lightening the intensity of what I want from her.

"What about-" she starts to ask with a pained look. "I need to talk about what happened," she says with tears in her eyes.

"It's over with, Hally," I shake my head, wanting that night to go back to not existing. Just pretend. It's what I had to do for so long. She can too. It makes living that much easier.

I silence her and ask her, "Can we just pretend?" I feel like an asshole. Like a coward. Like I don't fucking deserve my freedom. "Just forget it happened," I tell her and pray she'll play along. I can't make it right; there's no way to make it better. I wish I could for her. I'd give anything to go back and never tell her to go home in the first place. Then she wouldn't have done the one thing she knew would piss me off. She wouldn't have put herself in danger.

If that night had never happened, if so many little things had just gone differently, our paths would have been so divergent from where we are now. I don't think I ever would have left her.

She searches my eyes for something, I don't know what she's looking for, but whatever it is, it spurs her to rise up on her tiptoes and plant a small kiss on my lips. Her long lashes flutter open and she says, "I can." Then she chews on her bottom lip and her fingers comb through her hair as she looks away and I'm not so sure she's being honest. But what choice do I have?

"I just don't know if this is best, Nathan," she tells me the truth and it guts me. "I don't know if I can be around you and not ..." she doesn't finish, but I know exactly what she means. It's a constant reminder just being this close to her.

I shrug as if it doesn't shatter everything in me and say, "Just to talk, Hally." I almost don't say anything more, but I know she just needs a small push. "I miss you," I tell her and it's only then that I realize how much truth there is in those words.

"I miss you, too," she breathes the words so easily like they were waiting on the tip of her tongue to be confessed. "Okay," she says but then she chews the inside of her cheek nervously.

"Okay, what?" I ask her as someone knocks on her door. My blood fills with anxiety. I just need her to say yes.

"Okay to the talk," she answers shyly.

And that's all I need to rise from my chair and get out of her room before I keep pushing her until I'm taking too much. It's been too long and the last thing I want to do is make things worse for us. "Monday then," I tell her without looking back at her. Without touching her or even saying goodbye.

I open the door to find the girl who came in with Hally, the one named Lydia in the paperwork Mark gave me. I give her a tight smile and keep the door open for her. Her eyes are wide and assessing, but she simply says a polite thank you and doesn't ask questions. I can see she has them though. Everyone here does.

It's only when I close the door behind me that I can breathe. It's only then I even realize what I told her. It's only Saturday. Monday's too far away.

Chapter 12

Harlow

Margo Hawkins is striking. Her blunt bob is angled and severe; paired with her thick-rimmed chic glasses, she looks like a sexy librarian. Or maybe I just think that because of the notebook in her lap as she jots down notes during the interview.

I wring my fingers around one another nervously. My anxiety is getting the better of me, but I'm trying not to show it. It's an interview that was really meant for Julie ... and yet again, I've taken her spot.

"There are only four weeks to shoot the first season of *Night Fire* and with the sudden change of roles, you're demanded to work nearly fourteen hours a day, is that true?" she asks me, peeking up past her glasses and then flashing a gorgeous smile.

"Yes," I reply hesitantly. Time is blurring past me as I go through the motions. The only time I feel in control is when I'm on set. When I'm someone else.

"What's it like working with your former flame?" she asks me, catching me off guard even though I knew this question would be coming.

My lips twitch into a small smile and I let out a small laugh, although it's rehearsed and for good reason. "It's wonderful seeing Nathan again," I say easily as a blush creeps into my cheeks.

Margo cocks a brow at me and a few people whispering just outside of the green room where the interviews are conducted, catch my eyes.

"Is he the reason you got into acting?" she asks me, her pen poised and ready to take notes. "It seems like he played a major part in getting you this role."

I blink away the sleep from my eyes. I couldn't sleep last night because all I could think about was the past. It's been years since the nightmares have haunted me. But they've come back with a vengeance.

"I knew he was acting, obviously, but I never watched any of his movies." I stumble over my words and tuck a stray hair behind my ears. Scooting up in my seat I take a moment to clear my throat before answering, "I didn't expect him to be here, to be honest." I glance at the floor as I answer. It's a clean and bright walkway; nothing can hide on a floor like this. "It's not like I sought him out if that's what you're asking."

"It's not, but speaking of that, did you not ever reach out to him? This was all just a big surprise?"

She asks me as though it's not a coincidence, and it makes my heart race and my hands go numb. I never wanted to see him again when the visions of that night disappeared. I didn't want the reminder when I thought my life was normal once again. "I didn't. We thought it was best ..."

I swallow thickly and lick my lips, trying to pull myself together.

"I'm sorry dear, you must be exhausted from such a long day of work. And it looks like you didn't get much sleep," she adds with a bit of humor and a wink. I let out an uneasy laugh although I know what she's implying. I don't care though, I just want to get out of here and go hide.

"What was it like to go to school together?" Margo asks, maintaining her questioning about the relationship rather than the actual production, which is what Nancy assured me this would be about.

"I didn't know that was known," I answer as I tug my dress down a little farther and cross my ankles, but keep my knees touching. It was more for me than her, but before I can respond with any more she asks, "Oh, you don't want it out there? Is there a reason?"

My body heats. It feels like a fucking inquisition. I simply shake my head no, keeping my lips pinned shut. There's no way I'm giving this woman any more ammunition.

"Do you mind if I ask what was it like the last time you saw Nathan? Before filming?" She's seemingly sweet and unassuming in her questioning, but there's a vulture behind her eyes, waiting for the perfect time to swoop down and claim its kill. I can see it.

I bite the tip of my tongue for a moment before answering, "The last time I saw him was back in high school. I didn't think I'd ever see him again." I feign a sense of easiness, but the memory of him walking away steals the small smile from my lips. I can't help that it hurts. The emotions are etched so deeply and entrenched in my memories; they refuse to be ignored.

I shrug and say, "He was a year older, so I had another year to go before I could leave." I try to make it lighthearted and joking, but her next question destroys my attempt to sway the questioning.

"What happened that drove you two apart?"

She asks the question I didn't want to hear. But I'm prepared for it. I open my mouth to repeat the words, the script I've drilled into my brain for this particular moment.

My lips part and I take in a small breath, but the words are absent.

Fuck. I forget the lines.

"He did something that really hurt me." I shake my head no, closing my eyes and trying to remember anything about our past except that night. "That's not it, I'm sorry," I say and press my fingers into the lines creasing my forehead. "We didn't go well together. Always fighting and then I thought" Damn it. I wish I could just think of something. I open my eyes and see everyone watching. What did I already say? Shit, I can't remember.

"We broke up because we just weren't meant to be," I tell her and it shatters my composure. I don't lie. At least I try not to. But that's the worst lie I've ever told.

"Oh dear, I can tell this is hard for you," Margo says and plucks a tissue from the box beside her chair, passing it to me. "Take your time, Harlow," she says as she tilts her head with sympathy. Of the two of us, she's the better actress right now.

I was a dumbass to think this interview would be anything other than a predator prying for information to gossip about.

I shake my head and breathe out deeply before saying, "We were oil and water back in high school. All we did was fight. I can't remember what the last one was about." I shrug and add, "But we didn't get back together like we did all the times before."

"Oh, so you were on-again, off-again?" she asks and I nod, thankful that she's letting the question go. "I imagine that's the way it is dating the bad boy in high school."

I huff as I roll my eyes. I never thought of him that way. Not once. There was something else though. Something that crackled between us and drew me to him.

"He wasn't really a bad boy, to be honest. He was quiet and kept to himself," I say as I remember the first time I looked behind me in class. I can still feel his eyes on me and how he refused to let my gaze go. "There was an air about him that told me he was bad, but he didn't really get into trouble. He was just from the bad side of town; you know?"

I answer as if I'm talking to a friend, and that's a mistake.

"He was arrested though," she says as she places her pen down and pushes her glasses up the bridge of her nose. "I would say that's a bad thing, wouldn't you?"

"That was after we broke up," I say defensively.

It was months later that he started doing stupid shit. It was one fight after another once we split up. He was expelled after a fight that ended with the other kid's nose being broken. I found out later it was because Matt was talking shit about me. I thought maybe I could approach him then, but he'd never been colder to me than that day I showed up at his house.

Even worse, he got caught for stealing, not once but twice and the second time was when they locked him up. When I first saw him being arrested, I thought the cops had found out the truth, but turns out it was just petty theft and we'd gotten away with everything. It didn't make anything feel better; it didn't make anything right.

"Oh, is that so? Do you think the breakup had anything to do with his outbursts?" she asks and I don't have an answer.

Again, my mouth parts but the words just hang there,

refusing to leave me. I never thought about it like that. I remember thinking he wasn't the boy I loved. That he was someone else.

I never thought it was all an act.

Blinking away the memories and confusion, I start to tell her that we were just two young and dumb high school kids, to try and blow off her questioning, but when I raise my eyes I catch sight of him watching me.

The cold in his gaze is back and it sends a chill down my spine.

With that look, I know I've said something I shouldn't have, but I don't know what.

Chapter 13

Nathan

All I keep thinking about is Hally implying I wasn't a bad guy until I left her. You do stupid shit when you blame yourself and you're convinced you aren't worth a damn thing.

I think I wanted to get caught. I wanted to go to prison like the criminal I was. It made it easier to forgive myself for leaving her the way I did.

Fuck, some nights I prayed that she would tell someone so it could all just end. But she never did. That was the worst torture of them all.

Everyone around me, walking through the hall of dressing rooms, must know I'm pissed and I don't care. My hands are shoved in the pockets of the suit pants I'm wearing for the scene

I just did, and my tie is loose around my neck. I pace back and forth outside of her room waiting for her agent to leave.

The oxford shoes I got from the set stomp the floor as I walk, ignoring how everyone passes by me, each of them tearing their stare away from me as I look up from watching my feet hit the ground. Stomp, stomp, stomp. The steps are only dulled by the thick carpeting.

I'm sure Nancy is telling her that she needs to go into an interview more prepared than she was. Maybe it's Nancy's fault. She should have prepared her.

What's done is done, but the information she gave Margo is going to give me a fucking PR nightmare. My phone vibrates in my pocket and I check the name.

Mark.

To hell with that, I'm not taking it. There's only one person I want to talk to about that interview.

The sound of her door opening stops my feet right where they are and I turn to see Nancy taking a step down from the makeshift dressing room and easily closing the door behind her. She sees me when she lifts her head, simultaneously searching for something in her oversized bag. She gives me a smile as if everything's just fine and says, "Mr. Hart."

I watch her leave, knowing there's more going on behind the scenes and very much aware that she's a better actress than I gave her credit for.

I don't knock and I don't ask to come in, I barge in and

catch Hally by surprise. She jumps at her seat on the vanity, putting a hand to her heart as I close the door behind me.

"Nathan," she says with a bit of shock in her voice, but she doesn't look me in the eyes.

"What were you thinking?" I ask her, letting the anger out little by little, like the edge of an over boiled pot of water, climbing higher and higher until it's spilling and uncontainable.

"Excuse me?" she says with indignation.

"You made me look like an asshole," I tell her.

"I only told the truth," she says and narrows her eyes to watch me stalk closer to her. She's defensive right off the bat, ready to fight. Maybe it's a bad habit, maybe she really doesn't think there's a damn thing wrong with the impression she gave the papers.

"Is that what you want? You want them to hate me? Is this your way of getting back at me?" I ask her and it hurts to say it. I wouldn't blame her if she was trying to punish me for leaving her. What I did was wrong. There's no denying that.

"What was I supposed to do?" she asks as if it was all an innocent accident.

"Easy," I tell her as I grip the vanity and lean over her, "You keep talking, don't acknowledge the question." I'm very aware of how intimidating I look right now. If someone came in, they'd see I'm angry, hovering over her. But I don't care. I want to protect her, and *us* and what we had. And she's destroying any chance at that by being stupid.

"Maybe that works for you and your asshole persona but that wouldn't work for me," she practically spits at me. "I don't hide behind a smirk and bullshit."

"Is that what I do?" I ask her and cock a brow.

"You act like you're some hotshot who's made it and doesn't have to deal with the shit problems he creates and then gets mad when they come back and you finally have to deal with them." Her voice rises as she talks, filling with more and more emotion.

"Go ahead and get it all off your chest," I tell her, egging her on when I know I shouldn't. "Tell me what you really think," I scoff.

"You left me because you were a coward," she sneers at me and then seems to realize what she said. She instantly backs down as she steadies her breathing, her shoulders rising and falling. She doesn't look me in the eyes.

If I was a lesser man, I'd flinch from the venom in her tone.

"Is that really what you think of me?" I ask her, but I don't wait for an answer. She just said it to hurt me.

This is why we don't work together.

We push each other further and further just because we can. Driving each other into a darkness we're desperate to be pulled out of. The worst part is that we each want the other to save us, yet we're so damn willing to shove each other deeper into the abyss.

The realization takes the edge off my anger and I push from the desk, turning my back to her and running my hands through my hair as I stare at the ceiling. We were toxic for each other back then. *This* is toxic.

"Don't turn your back on me," Hally says with feigned strength and anger, but the underlying emotion is fear. Fear of loss.

"I don't deserve this, Nathan," she says and again, the anger has waned substantially, leaving vulnerability left in its place.

She's afraid I'll leave, but that's never fucking happening again. I can deal with the anger. I'll take it out on her a different way.

She grips my elbow and pulls me to face her and I let her. Staring down at her and containing everything I feel in this moment, all I can do is tell her, "You put a target on our past; you know that, don't you? You put a target on me and my background."

My voice is low and even and she wasn't expecting it.

"I didn't," she says and her voice croaks and she swallows instead of finishing.

"You did," I tell her as my anger raises, since she's smart enough to know better. I won't let her lie to me.

"I didn't mean to," she says as she stares back at me with contempt. "I didn't mean to, Nathan," she repeats and tries to calm herself down. She's a whirlwind of emotion, chaotic and unsure of herself. That's the Hally I know.

"I know you didn't," I tell her easily and it snaps her out of wherever she was in her head. I want to admonish her, tell her what she should have done and how she's better than that, but it's not what she needs. Not right now as her eyes get glossy with tears.

I don't hesitate, I wrap my arms around her small body and pull her into me. Her fight is gone, and it's my fault.

It's all my fault.

"I'm sorry," she whispers and then slowly, ever so slowly, wraps her hands around my waist and rests her head against my chest. Why does it feel so good to hold her close and know that my touch can soothe her?

It's not fair. We're set up to fail.

"Forgive me?" she asks weakly, and I can't take it. I'm the one who needs to be forgiven. I reach up and brush my fingers along her throat before cupping her chin in my hand.

My thumb brushes along her bottom lip as I let the words fade in the space between us. I'm the one who needs to be forgiven. For everything.

I'm slow as I lower my lips to hers, but she's quicker, desperate. And I love it. I love her when she does this. When she acts like she needs me more than she does her next breath.

"Lie down," I whisper against her lips, and she falls easily onto the bed, her hands still in my hair and her thighs parting for me. The heat crackles between us.

I watch as her eyes close and her lips part just slightly, her chest rising and falling in a frantic rhythm. This is how she's always given herself to me, with everything she has and full of vulnerability.

She's perfect.

I leave an open-mouth kiss on her throat, feeling her body move beneath me, pushing against me and wanting more. My hands move of their own accord, knowing every inch as if she'd never left. As if she's always belonged to me.

I unbutton her blouse slowly, my deft fingers slipping the buttons free one by one. Her hands trace along my knuckles as I do, her eyes glancing between my heated gaze and where my hands travel, slowly inching lower and lower. Her skin is soft and warm against my hands as I push the shirt aside and plant a small kiss and then another, lower and lower.

She writhes under me, arching her back and squirming and it makes me smile against her stomach.

"Nathan," she pleads with me, her neck bowed as her nails dig into my shoulders. It cracks my composure. I can try to do slow with Hally. Every chance in the past, I tried. But it's still impossible.

I'm quick to pull down her leggings and then take my shirt off, not caring when I hear the telltale sign of a button popping off from being too reckless. It doesn't matter. I'll be reckless so long as I can have her.

Her hands travel to her inner thighs and she whimpers with need. I love that sound; I've missed it more than I ever knew.

"Spread your legs wider," I tell her in a deep, rough voice, one I hardly recognize and it takes me back to when we were younger. When I felt like she was mine in every way.

Her eyes slowly open, pale blue and crystal clear and piercing through me as I unzip my pants and push them down, quickly stroking my hard cock.

It's the little things she does that drive me crazy. Like how she stares at my length and licks her lips. I rub the bead of precum over the tip of my dick and stroke myself again, wanting so badly to tell her to lick it off, but I'm too desperate to be inside her.

I need her more than anything.

Hovering over her, and bracing a forearm by her head, I move my cock between her slick folds, my head brushing against her opening and then up to her swollen nub.

"You're so fucking wet for me," I whisper in a calm voice. How? I don't know.

The moment she looks back at me, intent on answering, I slam all the way into her. I keep my eyes on her, watching how her mouth hangs open and a silent, strangled scream accompanies her pussy spasming around my dick.

I want to keep my eyes on her, to watch every movement and worship every small touch and desperate scratch she gives me, but I can't. It feels too good. I close my eyes and groan as I pull out quickly and then slam myself all the way back in, buried to the hilt and desperate for more, but afraid it will be over before I'm ready. I don't give her tight walls any time to accommodate me; I can't. I need her just like this. Rough and raw and completely at my mercy.

"Nathan," she breathes my name frantically, her walls tightening even more and making each thrust bring me closer and closer to cumming.

My toes curl and I pound into her over and over again, the small bed knocking against the wall each time. Her heels dig into my ass as she moans the sweetest noises, climbing higher and higher.

My balls are already drawing up, ready to spill myself deep inside of her. I reach between us, pressing hard against her clit and pinning her down as she tries to move away from the intense pleasure.

I don't let up on either the strumming of her clit or the steady ruthlessness of each hard stroke, filling her completely.

"Nathan!" she screams my name, her eyes wide open and staring straight at me as she cums on my dick. Yes!

I crash my lips against hers, silencing her and continuing my unforgiving rhythm, riding through the intensity of her orgasm.

I need more. More of her, of this, of us. I don't want it to end, but as she lets out a strangled moan and then gently kisses the dip in my throat, I can't hold back any longer. It's my undoing.

It only takes a few more strokes, each one harder and faster. I slam into her one last time, burying my head in the crook of her neck as hot streams leave me and my dick pulses deep inside of her.

A thin sheet of cold sweat covers my body as I lift my head and kiss her once, then twice on the lips. Her fingers spear through my hair and pull me in for one more. Our hot breath mingles between us and it's all I've ever wanted. Everything I've dreamed of for the last decade.

As our breathing calms, she nestles herself into the crook of my arm and all it does is make me want more of her. So many years I've had to live without her in my bed. When she should have been here all along.

I kiss her hair, trying to remember what she told Margo. It doesn't matter. It'll be twisted just enough to be convincing and enticing and I can read all about it in the gossip columns and trashy magazines tomorrow.

All I know is that the one good thing I ever had when I was a kid, is now going to be slandered. I deserve it all anyway. In one way or another. She doesn't though.

"I'm sorry for what I said," she says, letting me know she's thinking about it, too.

I kiss her hair again and clear the tightness in my throat before telling her, "I know what you said in the interview wasn't intentional. She baited you but you're smarter than that, Hally."

She tries to pull away from me and I give a little, only enough so that she grabs my forearms and looks up at me. "I said I was sorry," she tells me and then sniffles. "I'm sorry for what I said here too," she admits and then stares straight at my chest. "I don't know why I said that."

"Because I was a coward," I tell her. I can admit it. I was afraid. I convinced myself that she needed to be away from me because I was terrified of destroying her. "I'm sorry," I add.

"I didn't mean--" she starts to tell me, but then stops short, not wanting to fight again or to bring it up. A habit of hers.

I could ask her which part. In here, or in the interview. But I don't want to know. I want it all to go away. The thing about letting your anger slip out in the form of words is that they can't be taken back. All the hurt and pain inflicted will always be remembered.

And we're both guilty of that.

Chapter 14

Harlow

Ten years ago
November 10

The lightning bugs under the trees light up the night far more than I thought they would. Other than pale moonlight that's scattered by the remaining leaves, it's dark in the back of the car, but not nearly as dark as I imagined it would be. I thought there were more trees up here. It's been a long time since I've come up here to the running trails.

It's beautiful still.

It doesn't change the fact that my first time will be in the back of a car on Fairview Hill.

"Is it your first?" Nathan asks me. My heart races as Nathan sits up and pushes the front seat further up to give us room. We *planned this, but I'm still scared. It's stupid. It's just sex. But it'll change everything. I know it will. And I want Nathan to be my first and only. I love him. And even if he hasn't said it back, I know he loves me too.*

"Yeah," *I finally answer him in a breath, taking my eyes away from the scenery and then looking into his dark eyes. They seem lighter tonight for some reason.* "I've never had sex before," *I tell him as I prop up on my elbows.*

He licks his bottom lip at my answer but doesn't say anything else and it makes my heart pound harder and anxiety race through me.

"Don't worry," *he tells me gently as he leans down to rest his forehead against mine. He kisses me once, quick and chaste as he rubs his thumb along my jawline.* "I've got you." *He keeps telling me that and in my head, I imagine he really means that he loves me.*

We're sprawled out in the backseat. I hide my laugh under my hand as Nathan hits his head on the ceiling again as he tries to take his shirt off.

"Do we have to get all the way naked?" *I ask him and then try to play it off like it's not that serious. But I don't want to out here. Not with this much light and knowing someone else could come.*

"You want me to just pull your skirt up?" *he asks me and I feel stupid. I turn my head to stare at the backseat and try to shake off all these nerves.*

"Hey, we don't have to do this," *he tells me and that makes me feel even worse.*

I reach up and rest my wrists around the back of his neck. "I want to," I tell him honestly. I'm scared and I don't tell him that, but I truly and deeply want him. More than anything, I want him to have me any way I can give myself to him.

"You know I love you even if you don't want to?" he tells me, saying words I've wanted to hear for so long, as if they're natural to us. My chest warms with something I can't describe. I'm too vulnerable and emotional when it comes to Nathan, but it's all for him and I'll never hold anything back.

"Take two!" Stevens yells from my right, off the set and sitting in an oversized chair a few feet off the ground. From the corner of my eye, I can see the cameras panning and moving slowly as I stalk across the set. Letting my fingers trail along the hotel dresser, I continue the take.

It's supposed to be a cheap hotel and I lift up my fingers, circling my thumb along my pointer and middle finger, as if there was debris or dust along the wooden top before moving my eyes to Nathan.

It's our fourth scene today and we have two more after this.

The metal case in my hand is heavy. Earlier it was light because it was empty, but now it's filled with money I owe him. My lips curl into a smile as the irony dawns on me.

That we're playing parts, and he's blackmailing me.

I pick up the case and lay it on the dresser as I hear the bed creak, knowing he's getting up and walking toward me, although my character doesn't. I keep my eyes on the case and the clicks of the locks fill my ears as my thumbs slide the locks back.

He comes up behind me just as I open it, wrapping his hands around the back of my neck and my hip.

"It's all there?" he asks in a deep, rough voice I love. His hand is hot on my neck, commanding and I welcome it.

Out of instinct, my head falls back and my eyes slowly meet his. I swear my heart beats slower, or maybe it's just that time has slowed.

"It's all there," I murmur and my voice is soft, low, and full of emotion and I question it, wondering if it's loud enough for the mics. But the look in Nathan's eyes silences me.

My character has fallen in love, even though it means she's dead, but she's not the only one.

"Cut!" Stevens yells out and the dozen or so people standing just off the set clap as the lights slowly flicker on. "That's a wrap!"

The diner scene is next, but it's only a small part for me. I just need to walk by the window, sneaking a look in. Nathan will be shooting it until they get it perfect though. Handing off the money and getting each and every detail right.

Nathan relaxes his hands, although the one at my hip grips me first, forcing me to look at him. I have to blush as we share a glance. He's proud. I know that's the look in his eyes. It has to be. I clear my throat as I close the case and lock it. Everyone's already moving around us on the set and taking things down. These scenes are done and we're on to the next, no stopping or breaks. It's tough going from one to the next and so on, but I love it.

"Nathan," Jim, an assistant director and the man in charge of stunts, walks onto the set and steals Nathan away. He's just a few feet from me, but I feel robbed. I want that scene to continue. I want so much more right now.

I imagine Stevens will have me go first so I can be done for the day. It's been twelve hours of shooting so far today. Between these heels and all of the tension between Nathan and me, I'm ready for bed.

I wouldn't mind watching him though. The thought of doing just that makes me turn around and lean against the dresser, watching as he talks to one of the supporting directors. The young guy is animated and excited about the next scene. There's an explosion and I'd bet he's been waiting on it all day.

Now that the sun is setting, it's time for the big bang, so to speak.

I rock on my toes as I clear my throat, patiently waiting for Nathan to be done. He glances at me as I look at him and it makes me smile a bit. With a blush coloring my cheeks, I stretch out my shoulders but then look forward to see a group of women talking. Four of them huddled in a circle, and one is ballsy enough not to avert her glance as she covers her mouth and continues to talk.

Gossiping, I'm sure. The smile slips from my lips and an insecurity I haven't felt since college settles in my gut.

Everyone knows we've slept together.

And everyone's talking about it.

"We've got two hours till showtime!" I hear off to my right as the assistant director walks from the set, checking his watch and then looking back at the clipboard in his hands. Nathan's already walking over to me, finished with his conversation and finally having a break. Even if it is a small one.

"Mr. Hart!" a girl who's no doubt in her late teens or early twenties calls out, jogging across the concrete floor and onto the set. As her heels click and she almost stumbles, Nathan turns his attention to her. He's just being polite and courteous as he helps to steady her and she laughs off her clumsiness, but it doesn't help that raw churning in the pit of my stomach. "Could I have your autograph?" she asks and pushes a DVD and Sharpie pen into his hands.

I can hear his rough chuckle from all the way over here as he slips off the black marker cap. While he's looking down, the young woman looks at me and then quickly at the DVD, guilt written on her face.

It doesn't matter. Plenty of women fawn over him. They'd kill to be in my shoes. Even just to be an actress. Snagging Nathan would be the sweetest cherry on top.

Even if it's just for the weeks of shooting.

The thought is what breaks me, nearly making me sick. So much so that I don't see Nathan until he's standing right beside me, splaying his hand on my back.

"You alright?" he asks me and I try to appear fine, nodding my head and telling myself that what other people think doesn't matter. "You don't look like you're fine, Hally," he says as he takes another step closer to me, coming a little too close for just friends.

My eyes close as I take in a long, steadying breath trying to figure out what to say and what I want.

"It's just complicated." I finally settle on the truth and it hurts to even admit that much to him. I don't want to fight. Not in the least, and I'm terrified that admitting anything to him is going to kick off a conflict that will fracture what we have forever.

"Is it the girl?" he asks me. "You're going to have people asking for your autograph too, you know?" he says halfheartedly as if he's oblivious to the fact that she lit up from his simple touch.

"I don't want to talk about it," I tell him as I tilt my head and slip off the earring on my right ear. It's cheap jewelry and part of the costume. I've had them in almost all day and I'll have to put them back in tonight, but I've just realized how much they hurt. They're too heavy.

I slip off the other as Nathan takes a half-step back and

loosens the tie around his neck, clearing his throat. I imagine he wants to say something and doesn't, either because we're surrounded by people or because he doesn't want to fight either.

This isn't healthy, are the words on the tip of my tongue. There are only three weeks left though and once it's over, it'll be better for us to be over too.

Chapter 15

Nathan

I'm in over my head, but that's how it's always been with Hally.

"Good work today," Stevens tells me as I unfasten the top button of my dress shirt, making my way off the set and toward my room.

I pause and glance up at him. He's not a talker, like me in a lot of ways. "Thanks. I'll be here all week," I respond easily and with a bit of humor. I resume walking since he's already looking back down at his schedule or lines or whatever's in the stack of papers he's holding.

I take a covert look around, searching for Hally, but not seeing her in the scattering of people. Filming's almost over and a large number of people are gone. Still, a dozen or so always come to watch when we're shooting and Hally's usually one of them. My stride picks up speed and my gut churns, telling me something's wrong when I don't see her. She hasn't missed a single shoot yet.

Ignoring the gut reaction, I keep moving to my room. I'm keeping to myself and making a beeline for my dressing room, not that anyone dares approach me. Hally may have taken me out of my shell a bit and thrown me off my game, but I'm still not the socializing type and everyone knows it.

Maybe she's waiting for me. I know it's wishful thinking, but even as I open the door to my room, I'm picturing her on my bed, waiting for me to lose myself in her.

A low groan of satisfaction rumbles from the back of my throat as I imagine her like she was the other night, laid out for me and bared to me in every way. I'll never have my fill of her.

The memory vanishes as I take in my empty room and have to swallow the fact that she isn't here; she wasn't on set and I have no fucking clue where she is.

I don't like it. It's none of my damn business, but that's the very reason I don't like it. I don't have a claim to her and the instability between us makes me cling to her ... and usually her to me.

I'm quick as I unbutton the shirt completely, feeling suffocated by the crisp linen for the first time all day. I toss it carelessly on the floor and swing the door open on the armoire, looking for a plain cotton t-shirt and sweats to change into. I need a shower first though, something to relax me.

I need Hally.

It's when I toss the change of clothes across the room and onto my bed that I see what's changed in the dressing room.

Another article sits dead center on the coffee table. Right where Mark leaves my schedule every day.

I don't give a shit what it's about or what it says, since I'm sure Mark will tell me regardless, but the picture is enough to make me pick it up.

The memories come back to me as I stare down at an old picture of us, although I don't know how they got it. It's of us in school, in the cafeteria. Maybe a photo shoot from the yearbook, I don't know. But she's so happy sitting next to me. What's more is the smile on my face. She made me so happy. No one can deny that.

NOVEMBER 30

"I'll see you after class," I tell Hally and kiss the side of her head quickly, letting her waist go and watching everyone else file into class.

I'm supposed to be down the east hall for gym, but I like walking her here to the north hall for her algebra class. It's a little more time to hold her, to hear her babble about whatever's on her mind. I don't have to say shit; just being with her is enough to make her happy. And that alone makes me happy.

"I love you," she tells me, gripping onto my one hand with both of hers.

I haven't told her how I feel since that night, our first night.

I almost tell her I love her out of pure instinct, but it's hard to say the words. They lose their meaning when you say it too much. If my parents' split taught me anything, it's just that. I won't waste them in between classes and throw them around so easily. I'll show her how I feel, that matters more anyway.

"You make me so happy," I tell her and then feel like a dick. It's the truth, but she wants more.

"Please," she says and looks at me with a pleading expression in her eyes and I let out a sigh. "I just want to hear it," she tells me. I hate the hurt look on her face.

I give her a smile, the one she wants and bend down close to her ear, brushing her hair away and whisper, "I love you."

It makes her smile and then she gives me a quick peck on the cheek before running into her class. That's enough to keep the trace of happiness on my face, but it's not what I feel deep inside.

It's like I'm pretending to be someone else when I'm with her.

The bell rings as the thought hits me, and I turn to find myself alone in the hallway and late for class.

This version of me is someone I want to be. Someone not afraid to tell her what she wants to hear. They're just words anyway.

But it's not who I really am.

"Finally," I hear Mark before I see him, turning around with the article still in my hand. My heart races as if he'd caught me back then, lying to myself and to her and trying to be someone I wasn't.

"We have to talk," Mark says, shutting the door and I take the moment to release a breath I didn't know I was holding and toss the article onto the desk.

"Have a seat," Mark says and it catches me off guard. That sickness comes back to me as I pull out the chair from the vanity and he takes a seat opposite, dragging the chair for the desk over to me and quickly sitting down.

With his elbows on his knees and his fingers laced together, his thumbs tap against one another as he talks. It's a nervous habit I've noticed he has.

"So, Harlow May," he says, keeping his eyes on me and then swallowing.

"Just spit it out, Mark," I tell him as I sit back casually, ignoring how my heart's rhythm is fucked and every muscle in me wants to move. I stay perfectly still, expressionless. Giving him nothing and waiting for him to show his cards.

He can't know the truth. No one else knows.

Unless she told someone and that's why she's gone. I choke on the thought, unable to breathe or move as my blood runs cold. *She wouldn't do that.* I know my Hally; she wouldn't. She can't. It would ruin us both.

"So, you're seeing her now?" he asks me and I hold his gaze, willing my body to do something. Letting myself entertain the idea that this line of questioning must mean she hasn't told a soul.

I scratch a nonexistent itch at my jaw, stalling for time and debating on an answer. "We're potentially rekindling an old relationship." I keep it vague. I trust Mark, I do. But only so much.

"This relationship is causing a lot of questions," Mark says and then visibly swallows. He's antsy, fidgety.

"Like what?" I ask him without bothering to hide the irritation in my tone.

"Like why is she scared to talk about it?" he says low, his eyes darting between the floor beneath his feet and then back up to me.

I don't answer him for a long moment and the tense air becomes suffocating. "It was one interview," I tell him, like it's annoying. Like there's no truth to the perception that she's afraid.

"I didn't do anything to her," I add and then look away, toward the door wanting to escape. It's a lie. I didn't help her; I left her, I ruined the beautiful spirit she had.

I knew better than to be with her back then, but it's different now. Isn't it?

"I wasn't implying anything, Nate," Mark says, raising both of his hands and with a look in his eyes that begs me to believe him. "It just looks bad."

"What about now?" I raise my voice in frustration, shifting in my seat. "It's obvious that things are good between us. We're fine," I tell him.

"It's uncomfortable because you're under scrutiny now, which is never a good thing unless you have a plan."

"What's that mean?" I ask, hating how he's pussyfooting around. "Just tell me what's going on."

Every second that passes makes my body hotter, my muscles wind tighter. It feels like they're trying to take her away from me. I won't let it happen. Not again.

"It may seem like the relationship is forced in some ways. Like you have something on her and you're using that to your advantage."

"Shut your fucking mouth," I spit at him, quickly standing from my seat and sending the chair backward, slamming into the vanity. And for the first time since I've met Mark, he's quiet as he stares back at me.

"That's what people are saying?" I practically yell at him, pacing in a small area of the room. "I would never use her."

I start to defend us. I want to tell him that I love her and that she loves me. That she's with me because she loves me, which is more than any other person has ever shown me in my entire life. She's the only one.

"It's just the worst possible scenario. That you got her the part for ..." Mark doesn't finish.

"It's not true."

"No one's saying it is, and it's important for you to believe me when I say that I believe you." He holds my gaze, waiting for something from me, but my head is spinning, my hands are clenched and I feel like a caged animal.

I know better than to let my anger get the best of me, but I need her and I don't have a damn clue where she is.

"Why? Why would anyone even think that?" I ask him although I didn't mean to say the words out loud.

"The interview-"

"It was only one-" I interrupt but he's quick to interrupt me right back, not letting me stop him from telling me the truth.

"And moments on the set. When the scenes are done and she looks less than comfortable." He clears his throat and doesn't ask me for an explanation.

I don't have one that I can give him either.

It's hard hiding a secret that's damning. It's even harder having a reminder. I know she thinks about it. I do too.

"What can we do?" I finally ask him. This mess needs to be cleaned up, fast and preferably via a new story in the papers.

"No one's running with that idea yet, they're all waiting for ammunition," he tells me and I nod my head.

"She won't give them any," I tell him as if it's a promise I can make.

"We have a meeting."

"With who?" I ask defensively, ready to turn down whatever reporter has questions. I'll tell them what Mark says they need to hear, but I won't allow questions. They need to stay out of our business. And Hally needs coaching before she puts herself in that line of gunfire again.

"With Harlow and her agent," Mark answers, rising from his seat. "I think it's in your best interest," he adds and motions toward the door.

Chapter 16

Harlow

"Do you think I'm going to be fired?" I ask Lydia as I take in a deep breath and try to keep myself from getting sick. I've barely seen her this last week. Moving out of her dressing room and into mine changed our dynamic ... as did me getting the lead.

"Because you fucked your ex?" Lydia asks, cocking a brow like I'm ridiculous. Her dressing room is completely different from when I last saw it. I think she's spent more time shopping than she has on the set. Which makes sense since her scenes are finished and she doesn't have anything else to do.

She moves a bag from Neiman Marcus off the bed and sets it down on the floor, rummaging through it. "Sweetheart, if they fired everyone who slept together, there would be no one left to cast," she says jokingly and then looks up at me. "You're fine," she reassures me when she takes in my still-worried expression.

"It's a PR meeting, love. Everyone has them. You're going to be fine," she tells me again as she stands up with a small box in her hand. "I got you something," she says sweetly, barely containing a smile and holding out her hand.

"It's for you, take it," she says, shaking the small box.

"You really didn't have to do that," I tell her as the box falls into my palm. It's heavier than I thought it would be from the size of it. It's only a few inches wide and tall.

"Yes I did, crazy pants!" Lydia says and pulls her long hair up into a ponytail, but then lets it fall. "You got the freaking lead, so I should be throwing you a parade."

I let out a huff of a laugh and slowly unwrap the thick, pearly white wrapping. The box under the paper is simple. Nothing fancy, and it opens easily.

"It's nothing big really," Lydia says as I pull whatever it is out of the box. Her fingers fidget around the hem of her dress. "Just a trinket."

I flinch as a piece of it seems to pop off, and then stare at a heavy painted petal in my hand. It's a pale pink with gold around its edges and a stripe of white that fades in the center.

"Don't worry, they're magnetic," Lydia says quickly and takes the box from me, pouring it out and letting an owl-shaped bauble sit in my lap. It's colorful, decorated in shades of blue and gray with bright blue eyes.

"He has your eyes, huh?" she says and it makes me laugh. I answer her, "I guess so."

She picks up the owl and slips the petal back into place, blending it into the sculpture.

"Oh," I gasp and then realize that's what the owl is made up of, beautiful petals and flowers. Each edge gilded with gold and fitting perfectly next to each other. "It's beautiful," I whisper, our fingers brushing as she hands it back to me.

"It was in *Cosmo*'s unexpected gift ideas feature this month and the second I saw it, I thought of you."

"Because of the blue eyes?" I ask her jokingly.

"Because when it's not together, it looks like scattered petals that have fallen apart, but really when it's all put together, it's so beautiful and something you wouldn't have imagined."

Her answer stuns me, making all of my emotions come back tenfold. I am in love with this owl. Everything about it. At the same time, I wish I had something to give her in return.

"Thank you," I tell her and wrap my arms around her even though I'm still sitting down.

Lydia shrugs, straightening herself and downplaying how sweet her gesture is. "My credit card was burning a hole in my pocket," she says and winks.

"I owe you big time," I answer her, gathering the pieces and putting them back in the box.

"Remember me when you're famous, will ya?" she asks me and it makes me laugh. A real laugh that shakes my shoulders.

"It's good to see you smile again," Lydia says softly and her expression changes, with nothing but sincerity on her face.

"You love him?" she asks me gently at the same time her phone goes off. An annoyed look replaces the soft smile as she silences it. "I was worried at first," she tells me, slipping the phone into her pocket and then looking back at me. "But now I get it."

I don't answer her, not trusting that I can even form a coherent sentence. It's amazing what just one person whose understanding and support you have feels like. How much weight is lifted.

"I have to go, but I don't want to leave you," she says with a guilty tone in her voice.

"I'll be fine," I tell her more to ease her worry than to be truthful.

She's the one, this time, to give me a death grip hug.

When she releases me, she whispers, "Go, get out of here and see what the hell they want you to do."

"Maybe it's a shampoo commercial," she adds with a smirk on her lips.

I playfully smack her arm. "Shut up," I say jokingly and shake my head.

I know I'm already late and an emotional wreck, but at least I'm a little more lighthearted.

"I'll see you when I'm done."

"I have to check out and I don't think my card will be active," she tells me, the humor and playfulness gone. "I won't go far and the minute you need me, call and I'm here."

I nod my head, hating that she's leaving and feeling more and more alone.

"Got it," I tell her and give her one more hug. "Thank you for everything," I say, squeezing her tight.

"Just remember," she says before she leaves, "Everything happens for a reason."

Chapter 17

Nathan

St. Gerard's corporate rooms are exquisite; it's obvious they spared no expense. From the beveled glass, mirrored pendant chandelier in the center of the room, to the coffered ceiling with disguised recess lights, everything reeks of wealth. The combination of the lighting creates reflections across the slick, dark mahogany table that takes up the entirety of the expansive room.

It's gorgeous and meant to aid in getting deals done.

But with only four people in the sweeping space, it feels cold. Especially so as I stare across the dark table at Hally, who's struggling to look me in the eye.

I crack my knuckles one at a time, listening to Nancy talk

as she sifts through a stack of printed papers in front of her. Each an article or mention in a gossip column. Mixed in are photos of us that were leaked online from back in high school. Those are the only ones I even bother to look at.

"As I discussed with my client, her interview is causing a little speculation," Nancy's voice changes, strengthening and ringing clear in the large room. My eyes shift from Hally's to hers.

I shrug my right shoulder and rest my forearm on the table. "I'm sure it'll blow over."

I give my response at the same time Hally says, "I'm sorry." Her eyes dart everywhere like she's in trouble. Her hands are beneath the table, and I can only imagine she's toying with the hem of the shirt she's wearing. It's black with a deep V but more importantly, it's almost sheer and in this lighting, I can make out the lace of her bra.

I imagine it was for the set because it's not a shirt I could see Hally wearing. But then again, I haven't seen Hally in her own clothes, or have I?

The inner thought makes my brow furrow and right then she glances at me.

"This is on the cusp of very good or very bad," Nancy says but I refuse to break Hally's gaze. She's scared and that fact is terrifying me.

All she has to do is forget. For the love of God, if she could just forget what happened, everything would be perfect.

"I don't want to hurt his career," Hally says hesitantly,

breaking eye contact with me, her voice lowering toward the end.

"Relax," I tell her at the same time that Mark starts to talk. He stops when he hears me, waiting to see if I have more, but I don't. I just listen to what they say and abide by it.

I motion for him to go on and he says, "I know you're new to this Miss May, but everything's going to be just fine. We're here for precautionary reasons."

Nancy nods her head and adds, "We're paid to prevent the bad times from ever happening."

"What's the story between you two? You need to tell us if anything could be revealed that would cause ... issues," she says, making small circles with her hand in the air.

Hally's quiet, so I answer for her.

"We had a rough breakup." That's as simple as it gets.

The room is quiet for a second too long, the tension growing.

"So, it was rough seeing him again," Mark prompts Hally, but then Nancy cuts him off.

"You could quit right now on this set and there's so much buzz around this that I could get you another gig like that," Nancy says to Hally and snaps her fingers, although I'm sure it's solely for my benefit, since it's obvious the two of them have already talked.

"How are we spinning this?" Mark asks and it pisses me off. They're blowing everything out of proportion.

"It was just one shaky interview," I say and I don't hide the irritation in my voice.

Nancy tosses a stack of pictures down in front of me, several taken throughout the last two weeks. She straightens one in front of me so I can see it clearly. It's at eye level, obviously taken with a cell phone.

"And it's just a picture, right?" she asks rhetorically as I take in a long breath. My fingers itch to touch the edge of the picture. Hally's eyes stare at my back in the photo, every emotion on her face visible. I scan the rest of the photo, but it wasn't taken on set. That's more than obvious and my blood freezes as the easiness of my posture hardens.

She's terrified.

"Pictures say a thousand words, and this one says that he broke your heart ... for a reason," Nancy says.

"And that reason doesn't matter," Mark says and sits straighter in his seat. "Everyone loves a second chance."

Nancy's smile turns coy and then she looks at Hally, who's focusing on the picture that's sitting in front of me.

She's been telling me she wants to talk. I know she has, and yet, I've put it off.

Why can't she just forget? Why can't she pretend it didn't happen?

I nod my head at Mark's suggestion, waiting for Hally's reaction. She's quiet and unresponsive.

I sit up in my seat as Mark and Nancy talk about how the two of us dating is the gossip that everyone will want. They go on about planning dates and discussing where exactly we should be seen. They'll plan it all out and give us the script.

We can handle that much. But the longer I sit here, willing Hally to look at me, the worse and worse the sickness in my stomach gets.

"So, what happened in high school that made you break up?" Mark asks and the question rouses Hally, but she doesn't answer. Instead, she looks back at him with something that shatters my heart. Guilt.

I'm a dick for doing it, but I give her an out. I hand it over to her, ready to let her be free of all of this shit. "Why don't I let Hally tell you?"

Hally's lips turn up into a small smile as she wipes tears from the corners of her eyes. Nancy pulls on the crook of her elbow and whispers in her ear, but Hally shakes her head. I watch it all like a bystander, as if I can't help what's about to happen.

"Did you know Nathan's the only person to ever call me Hally?" she says softly as Nancy lets go of her. She looks at her fingers as she wipes a bit of black from them, I'm guessing from her mascara.

"I've noticed," Nancy says, eyeing Hally and waiting for more.

"I made him," she says and then lets out a sad laugh. "I didn't want him to call me the same name everyone else did." She forces her tears back and takes in a steadying breath. "I knew there was something between us instantly."

"Love at first sight?" Nancy says as she jots something down on the back of one of the papers.

"Some would call it that," Hally says.

"Would you?" Mark asks and Hally nods her head.

My heart hammers in my chest, too hot and too full of raw emotion to settle into place.

"But we were like oil and water; that's the saying, right?" she asks and then looks up at me. "We picked fights for no reason, both of us hotheaded and unwilling to be wrong."

"Young love," Mark says beneath his breath and Nancy nods, jotting that down too.

"Young and stupid," Hally says and I hate it. We may have been, but that night is what she's thinking of. I can see it in her eyes.

"I was stupid," I interrupt her and Hally finally looks up at me, shaking her head slightly.

She swallows and almost says something. She almost contradicts me, but then bites down on her words. She doesn't want to fight me, and I hate it. My hand clenches into a fist on the table, feeling like I'm losing her.

"And you broke up, over the fighting, we'll say," Nancy says as the silence stretches for too long. "Now what was on your mind when you saw him, Hally?" Nancy asks and my body stills, my lungs refusing to fill.

How could I not have noticed? I glance back down at her picture. How was I so blind to her pain? I put my elbow on the table and my chin in my hand. Covering my mouth with my fingers I keep my emotions in check, waiting for Hally to answer.

"I was scared," she says with a nod and then another, the second one more confident. I can see it in her eyes that she wants to tell them the truth.

She's sweet and naïve, so it's only a matter of time before she slips. In this industry, they never let up.

Before they can ask her why, she gives a small smile and says, "I thought he wouldn't want me the way I wanted him." Her voice is hopeful and filled with nostalgia.

Even I would believe her, if I didn't know it was a lie.

She was scared of our past, of that night. The reminder and the pain it carries.

"Now, Nate, you need to remember these details," Nancy says and it pisses me off.

"Easy enough since it's all true," I snap back at her. They think it's a lie? A charade? I don't care.

The only thing I care about is the fact that she's hurting and I've been ignoring it.

There's one person who could destroy me and she's the one I'm giving everything to.

Chapter 18

Harlow

Ten years ago
April 12

Nina's is an old mom and pop type place on the corner. It's a little Italian restaurant on Fourth Street, small and right on the edge of the rough part of town, but it's where we used to go on Fridays. They had five dollar pizzas and dollar drinks. It was cheap and a habit we got into.

It's also where we were when it started, when I decided to be an idiot. Really, I just wanted to piss him off. I think that's what kids do when they're in love and hurt. They lash out. I know better now, or at least I like to pretend I do. But back then, I just wanted him to regret throwing away what we had. It was foolish and it's why I think it was all my fault.

"I want to tell my parents," I tell him again. I swear he's ignoring me, and it's pissing me off. He knows how important this is to me. It's eating me alive.

We had sex. We've really been having sex regularly. Every time I see him. Every fight we get into. All I want to do is kiss him and then more.

Last night was my breaking point. I sneaked out and met Nathan at the corner store. He didn't hesitate to buy the box of condoms, even with me standing right there. I held his hand with both of mine and tried to pretend it was okay, but it wasn't.

Miss Andrews was at the register and she knows my mother by first name. I don't want my parents to find out because of someone else. Instead of bringing it up last night, we fought about him buying the condoms and then used them in the backseat of his car.

Some backbone I have.

I have to admit; I like it though. I like people knowing. I like him having me whenever he wants. Wherever he wants. Even if that makes me dirty. But I don't want people to think of me that way and definitely not my parents. I can't have them finding out from someone else.

"Then tell them," he answers me, but he doesn't elaborate.

"Are you coming with me?" I ask him. I don't want to do it alone. I'm practically terrified. I think they already know though,

but I'm not sure.

"Fuck no," Nathan says and looks back at me like I'm crazy.

"Well, I don't want to do it alone." I try not to raise my voice, but I do. It makes my heart beat faster thinking someone heard. I look over my shoulder from our booth in the corner but no one's looking at us. The only other people in here are a few guys who just got off work at the steel mill, or maybe they're on their break, I don't know. But they're all in the opposite booth and the one right next to it. Dirty boots and the thick jackets with Stanley's Steel logos give away who they are.

"You don't need me there," Nathan says and then wipes pizza sauce from his hand with a thin napkin. He balls up the napkin as I answer, "I do. I want you there." I try to put as much sincerity as I can into my tone.

"That's not happening," he tells me as though it's final.

"Because you don't want to and what I want doesn't matter?" I ask him with nothing but venom.

"I can't deal with this right now," Nathan tells me, brushing me off. He makes me feel like I'm the crazy one.

"Is it that big of a deal to be by my side when I tell them?" I ask him desperately. Nathan looks at me for a moment like he's considering what to say, but then he just looks out of the window as a car passes, completely distracted and not actually participating. That's all I want; is it that unreasonable?

"So what?" I ask him, throwing my hands into the air and leaning back against the booth. The cheap vinyl squeaks and

protests. I hate this little restaurant. The tables are cheap; the flooring is peeling.

"So, drop it."

I flinch at his blunt response. I don't like living like this, feeling as though I'm lying.

"They don't even know we're dating, let alone how serious it is," I tell him as if it's a confession. It really is, for me. I feel guilty and just want it off my chest.

"Is it really that serious?" he asks me like I'm being dramatic.

I sit there dumbfounded, falling back into my seat as my blood turns cold. I try to clear my throat, but it's dry so I pick up the plastic cup of Coke and take a sip and then another, staring out of the large bay window and watching the cars drive by too. I ignore the pain in my chest and the way my eyes sting.

We're over. I won't give myself to someone who won't do the same in return.

But I already have, and that's the part that hurts the most. Young and dumb, puppy love. Whatever it's called, it's a brutal bitch.

It was a similar breakup, like so many that we'd gone through. At the time, it felt like the worst thing imaginable. Like he'd taken my heart and torn it to shreds and didn't give a damn about it.

So I stormed off. Determined to piss him off and get

under his skin like he'd gotten under mine.

I went down Rodney Street, making sure to take the first few streets I'd normally walk down on the way to my house. Just in case Nathan was watching. And then I went left, down *his* street. Into *his* territory.

I remember gritting my teeth and feeling so vindicated. He didn't want to date me, fine. He wasn't going to tell me what to do then.

I was in my boots and a flimsy sweater, not nearly warm enough for the weather and I cursed Nathan under my breath, not bothering to look where I was going or to notice how the people on the streets were disappearing, leaving the sidewalks vacant.

I looked up to see a street light flicker, the only one that was lit on that side of the street.

And then it happened. Chills cover my arms as I remember.

His hands were cold and rough as he pulled me just inside the alley. My heart slammed as I screamed out in surprise. His breath smelled like cigarettes. I tried to get away, I scrapped and screamed again, but I didn't have to try hard.

It was over so quickly. That's the part that was so utterly shocking. It only took one motion, one swift pull and shove from Nathan. The man flew back as Nathan ripped him away, tearing his fingers from under my sweater, his dirty nails scratching my skin as he was snatched away.

I heard a cry, my shrill scream from the terror I hadn't

realized was over. And then a crack. The sound is so pure in my head. A skull crashing against the sharp corner of a dumpster.

Crack.

It silenced me. It made the chaos go still. Somehow, deep inside, I knew it was all over from that sound. As if it were deeply embedded in me to know it was the sound that comes with immediate death.

So many questions rushed me. I kept wondering if it was real. Did it really happen?

Nathan dragged me down the street as I barely managed to keep up with him. Towing me by the arm and asking me over and over if I was okay. Physically I was fine; emotionally I was shaken, but I couldn't answer him.

Maybe I was in shock. I don't know, but when we stopped in front of the liquor store I stumbled and tried to figure out why we were there.

"The cops are coming," he told me.

My voice was caught in my throat. "Say something!" Nathan screamed as he shook me and although my memory is biased, I swear I saw fear.

"He's dead?" The words somehow slipped out.

Nathan stared at me as the realization dawned on me.

"They'll never know you had anything to do with it," he told me and then he let go of my hand. He ran a hand down the side of my face and now I know he was saying goodbye, one last touch, but I didn't understand it back then. I tried to hold his hand as he lowered it, but he pulled it away.

"You need to leave, Hally."

I stared up at him, dumbfounded and unsteady.

But the man was dead, the cops were here and I was looking into the cold eyes of the boy I loved so much. I'd never felt more alone and guilty in my entire life.

Chapter 19

NATHAN

I never dared to dream I could have her again. Not after I was so cold to her and distanced myself so completely. And now all I can see is her slowly slipping away from me after the way she acted in that meeting.

Our strides are in unison as we walk toward her dressing room, but I grab her hand with mine and keep moving, and she follows me. Just that acknowledgement is enough for me to wrap my arm around her waist, bringing her closer to me and holding her right where she belongs.

Next to me.

I had my reason for killing that piece of shit already in place before the cops even got there. I was going to tell them the dumb fuck had tried to mug me, and I hadn't meant to kill him. I was pretty sure I'd still serve time, even without any priors, but she had nothing to do with it and I would never let her get caught up in the shit life I led.

It was the only way I saw her getting away from it. She had to get away from me.

I open the dressing room door in a swift movement and wait for Hally before I step in, closing the door and locking it immediately.

I need to hold her, comfort her, hear whatever she's thinking. I tell myself that as I stare at the doorknob and prepare to turn around and face her.

I'm guiltridden all over again and I know the easy thing to do is just leave. But there's no good that can come from that. Back then, it made sense to a stupid boy who was scared but didn't want someone he loved to go down with him.

Times have changed and I need to make it right, but I don't know how. How could she ever forgive me?

"Is it just for the cameras?" Hally asks me. The chair to the desk rocks on its front legs as she pushes it slightly from behind. She doesn't look me in the eyes as she clenches her jaw, waiting for an answer.

"What are you talking about?" I ask her out of pure shock. That's not at all what I expected to come out of her mouth. I approach her slowly, but she squares her shoulders and looks back at me defensively.

"You said today, you'd do it to get them off your back," she says again, not looking at me and instead looking at the door. My heartbeat picks up. It's just like before. A massive fight over nothing and then she'll run. I can feel it coming.

"*Our* backs," I tell her and finally she looks up at me, but it's with daggers.

"You said *yours*," she says as her nostrils flare.

"I'm used to being alone," I answer her. "It was a-" she cuts me off right before the word "mistake."

"Is that what you want?"

"If I wanted to be alone, I would be," I tell her with a deathly low voice and take a chance moving closer to her. She backs away slightly, like my touch would burn her so I stop short. Hating that she's doing this.

"You know what I mean," she says. "Do you want me, or do you just want to fuck and smile for the cameras?" she says again and then adds, "You didn't answer me." She scoffs and then looks at the ceiling. "I guess that should tell me the answer right there." She's trying to play it off like she's foolish, but the pain causes her eyes to go glossy with tears.

How could she even question that? "I want you," I tell her simply. Hoping she'll drop the entire conversation and this agenda to end what's between us.

"So you really want to be with me?" she asks me like she doesn't believe me.

"Yes!" I yell louder than I should. If anyone is just outside the door, I know they can hear. I lower my voice. "Of course I want you." The words leave my lips and they're the truest and purest I've ever spoken.

"Then why didn't you say that? Why not just tell the truth?"

"What truth?" I ask her, bewildered.

"Today!" she yells, not caring in the least about anyone listening. "You could have told them we were together. You could have told them anything but instead, you just left me there ... alone."

"Where the hell are you getting this from?" I don't understand why this is even a conversation between us. I can't stand it. I ask the one question that matters. The one we should be discussing. "What are you afraid of, Hally?" I yell it out so loud it burns my throat, making it feel raw and dry.

"Of you," she says so low I almost don't hear her, her shoulders hunching slightly as her composure crumbles.

My body's still, in disbelief.

"Because you're going to hurt me," she says and slowly I regain my sense of control. I would never hurt her in any way. Ever. She has to know that. This is just bullshit she's spewing to push me away.

"I would never-"

"You left me," she whispers. "And it still hurts."

"I didn't ever want to hurt you," I tell her. "You have to know that."

"I don't know that," she tells me, her eyes brimming with

sincerity. "I needed someone," she whispers her choked words. "I still need someone."

"I'm right here, you can tell me anything," I say and my words are desperate. "Whatever you need to tell me, I'm here."

Tears leak down her cheeks and she wipes them away angrily. Like she's ashamed to have them show. "I don't know what to say; I don't know what I need." She shakes her head chaotically and I pray she just gives me something I can work with. A single thread to hold onto.

"Just tell me what's on your mind."

"What if it's just too late?" she asks me, not quite a question and more of an accusation. One well earned on my part.

"It's not," I tell her with complete sincerity. I can't turn back time, but it can't be too late. Every moment I have to live is a moment I can try to make it right. I just don't know how.

"What happens after filming is over?" she asks me. "That's a question," she says like she has me cornered. I could play dumb and avoid the conversation, or bring up the fact that we'll both be asked back next year so long as the ratings are what they should be. But I know what she's referring to and I don't have an answer for her.

"I don't know, Hally." I'm slow with my words, careful. My head is spinning and I don't know what she wants to hear.

"I need something, Nathan." My mouth hangs open a moment and then I slam it shut.

I almost ask her what she wants, because I'd give it to her, whatever it is. But she doesn't give me the chance.

"I loved you," she says with pain as if it's a sin to say the words.

Loved. As in past tense.

My blood goes cold and I wait for whatever she's going to say next. How she'll throw it in my face that I never loved her back. I know it's coming. I'll take it. I swallow the lump in my throat, staring back at her and waiting for the assault.

She can berate me, hate me, blame me—whatever she needs, so long as she doesn't leave.

As if she's heard my thoughts, as if knowing what would hurt me most, she pulls herself together enough to look me in the eyes.

"I have to go," Hally utters hurriedly, stepping around me and my first instinct is to cage her in. One palm against the wall and her chest to mine, I do it.

"Don't," I tell her, gritting my teeth and forcing the word out. She looks me in the eyes and moves under my arm. My body's frozen in place. I can't keep her here. I can't hold her against her will.

"Don't leave, Hally," I tell her with as much strength as I can manage.

"I need time to think about it all. I just can't-" she starts to say and then Hally pushes past me. As I try to grab her hand, she rips herself away from me.

She doesn't finish her thought; she doesn't say goodbye.

She just leaves me alone and it's the worst feeling in the world.

It's the feeling that I shouldn't go after her.

The feeling that I never deserved her.

The feeling that she's not going to come back.

"She will," I mutter beneath my breath. She's just scared. But she'll come back. Or I'll go get her. One way or the other, I'm not letting her get away from me again.

Chapter 20

Harlow

"Once more!" Stevens yells out and I look back at him, my eyes stinging from a night of letting it all out. Today's the last day of shooting and thank God I only need to walk and look into a window while another actor, a side character, counts the cash.

It's a simple task, but Stevens keeps recording. Repeatedly. Unceasingly. He's been a pain in my ass this last week. Maybe that's one more thing that's been picking at me. It's like he can see it too. Maybe it's written on my face. Maybe they can all hear what I'm screaming inside my head.

I knew I had to end it before we even got back to his dressing room. Article after article couldn't have convinced me. It hurt to read them, each one chipping away at my armor little by little. But that's not what did me in.

He could never say it back to me. I love you.

Not then, and not now.

It's because he doesn't really love me. I'm foolish to think he does. You don't throw someone away if you truly care about them. Not when they're hurting and so thoroughly destroyed.

I didn't know what a fucking mess I was until I saw that look in my eyes in that picture. It's brutal to have the truth plastered in front of your face. The fear and stupidity, really.

He makes me weak.

And I'm done with being anything less than the strong woman I've set out to be.

I wait for my cue, rocking on my heels as the click of the safe closing is followed by, "Action!"

Three, two, and one. I start walking. Three steps past the darkened window and I take a glance inside, just a small one, as if I was only a passing bystander. My heels click with my easy strides and the red scarf over my head tickles at my ears as I move, but I don't touch it. I refuse to let my face move either. Even as I leave the window and wait quietly on the edge of the set, watching as the cameras continue to roll.

Stevens has four of them going now. How many angles does he need?

I grit my teeth, hating how irritable I am. I'd rather be angry. Anger is so much easier to hide.

"You alright?" a small voice from my right asks and I snap out of it, looking at an extra I recognize.

"Yeah," I reply and shake my head and give her a smile. Her name's Rachel, or her character's name is. Shit, I forget.

"It's a wrap!" she says with a smile and humor although her face is still scrunched, and the humor doesn't reach her eyes. She keeps walking ahead of me and that's when I notice the set is clearing out.

An uneasy breath leaves me as I reach down and take off the heels one at a time. My bare feet hit the cement floor as the backdrop is lowered by the stage crew.

I force a smile on my face and keep in mind that today is over. This entire ordeal is over.

We have a one-week break before we hear back about any alterations or retakes. A full week of being away from Nathan. And if I want, Nancy's assured me that I never have to see him again.

I try to ignore the pain from that thought as I walk through an empty hall back to my room. It's what I wanted, what I demanded, but that only makes my heart clench harder.

The second I close the door; I hear my phone vibrating on the desk. I sag against the door, leaning my head back and staring at it.

Let it ring.

I imagine it's my mom again. Telling me to come home. Telling me she's worried for me.

I'm worried too. But I don't want to run and hide away. I don't want to go back to what I was before this, but I don't know where I can go from here.

I slowly lower myself to the floor and as my ass hits it, my phone vibrates again.

I just want to be left alone.

But what if it's Nathan? My heart slams and I quickly scramble to get up. I won't answer, I just want to know if it's him. He messaged last night, and I was able to control myself. But now I'm like a junkie, eager to see if he still wants me.

Thoughts and accusations ricochet in my head, whispering that I'm weak, but I ignore them. Only to swallow my own pathetic wishes when I see it is just my mother. I can't talk to her right now. Not when I don't have a plan. She wants to protect me and take care of everything for me and I know she loves me, but I don't want to live in a bubble all my life. I love her, and she knows that, but I need to live my own life.

I toss my phone onto the desk and it hits the edge of the stack of papers Nancy gave me. I glance at the top one.

PAGE SIX OF THE NEW YORK POST

Is it over before it even started?

That's what fans of the now-lovebirds Nathan Hart and Harlow May are wondering.

According to those close to the pair, Harlow's just a sweet girl caught up in the bright lights of the set and swept away by her former high school sweetheart.

But the feelings aren't mutual, sources say. He hasn't done a single thing to show his commitment and close friends know that the "dating" label is only to save face. She's naïve to think he still wants her. It's a relationship of convenience for him. The moment production wraps up, he'll be on to the next pretty little thing. There's nothing that indicates otherwise.

Seems like Mr. Hart isn't quite the sweetheart she remembered and he's only passing the time with Miss May.

It's the same one that was on the table when I walked into the conference room.

Humiliated. That's how I feel. Easily summed up into one word.

Even the rest of the world knows that I'm stupid. It's written in black and white. Of course it's convenient for him to put up with me rather than deal with the mess.

Isn't that what he's always done? Stupid. I've always been stupid and it seems like it will never change.

"I'm only stupid when it comes to him," I say under my breath.

I clear my throat and turn off vibrate on my phone. My head's killing me from lack of sleep. My body, in general, is exhausted. I'm emotionally a wreck.

Emotional is not a substantial enough word. What's wrong with me?

My throat gets tight as I set the phone down and I see a message from Nathan pop up. *Are you done?*

A warmth flows through me, almost relaxing. As if knowing he's thinking of me eases some of the pain etched deeply into my soul.

He texts me again before I can justify texting him back. *I want to see you before you leave.*

It's easier to just cut things off and run.

It's what he did to me and I understand why.

If I see him, I'll cave.

So instead, I run.

Chapter 21

Nathan

"If you break your phone, I'm not buying you another," Mark says from across the conference room. The signed contracts for upcoming promotions are the only papers on the twelve-foot-long table. He leans back in his seat, seemingly casual, but I know him better.

I try to respond with something, anything, but no words come to mind. I can't think about anything other than Hally. This meeting is the only thing that kept me from watching her today. That, and the fact that she told me she needed space.

That's a new one from her and it's a cruel one too. Because it gives me too much hope.

"You've been tense all day," he says to break up the silence.

"Are we done here?" I ask him, pocketing my phone and intent on going straight to Hally's dressing room. I pick up the pen, set it down on the stack of papers and push them forward, closer to him, although there's no way he'd be able to reach them. It's just to signify that I'm done with this.

He lets out an uncomfortable sigh, pulling at his tie and focusing on the checkered pattern before looking back up at me. "Is it Harlow?" he asks.

Shame is the first thing I feel and it's what makes me break his gaze. I can't look anyone in the eye, knowing I've lost her again. And it's my fault, I know it is. I've shut her down time and time again. There's only so much a person can take.

I should have been there for her years ago. Just like I've been doing all day, I take my phone out and see that she's seen the messages, but she hasn't responded.

The dry ache in my throat and the plummeting in my chest overwhelm the anger.

This isn't a stupid high school game. We've both grown up.

This isn't a fight either; I know how Hally approaches them.

She doesn't want me.

Plain and simple.

I know how I messed up. I just don't know how to make her forgive me.

"If you two split," Mark interrupts my thoughts and my eyes rise to his. I forgot he was even here. I forgot where I was. "We'll lose this deal. Well, one of the two of you will. There's no way they'll believe you can work together," Mark says and then cuts off his words. As if he's just now realizing I'm pissed off.

"What I was saying," Mark continues, shifting in his seat. "We have plenty of new deals available."

I tap my fingers on the table, the rest of my body like a stone. I don't even think I can repeat back what he said beyond the words, "*If you two split.*"

"We're not breaking up," I answer him simply. Denial. I hear the sinister whisper in the back of my skull, but I ignore it. "It's just a fight," I tell him although the excuse is more for me.

"And what's this fight about?" he asks.

I hesitate, and he takes the time to explain. "I've never seen you like this," he says.

"And?" I dare him to continue.

I can practically see the wheels turning in his head, wondering whether or not he should tell me what's on his mind.

"This isn't you," Mark suggests, gesturing with his hand.

I haven't been myself in years. I forgot who I was. And that's the way I wanted it to be. "The only person who truly knows me is her, Mark," I tell him and the raw honesty hurts.

She knows every flaw and every weakness. And she's never exploited them. She's loved me in spite of it all. My eyes close and my head falls back as I realize I haven't told her how much it means to me. How everything else could vanish and if only she was left, I would still feel complete.

She should know that, shouldn't she?

If there's one thing I should tell her, it should be that.

"Where are you going?" Mark asks me.

"To her room," I answer him quickly and dare him to question it.

His eyes narrow as he tilts his head. "Is she really worth it?" he asks and it's the worst fucking thing he could have done. My knuckles crack as I make two fists and push them against the table as I lean forward to answer him, holding back my rage and the desire to destroy him for questioning how much I love her. How much I need her. I wasn't even living until she came back to me.

"She is *mine*. My girlfriend, or whatever you want to call it. She's mine and I'm not letting her go," I tell him and my words come out more menacing than anything else.

He doesn't answer me for a long time, and I can see he wants to question me.

"I messed up. But it was ten years ago." My voice is raw as I tell him the truth, the full confession so close to the tip of my tongue. "How long do I have to pay for it?" I ask him as my heart feels like it's collapsing in on itself. "How do I make it right?" I barely get out as my breathing gets heavier, faster. I'm truly begging. I've never begged for anything, but for her, I'd do anything.

"Did you tell her you were sorry?" he asks me, the questioning in his eyes long gone. I nod my head in response, trying to relax my anxious body. "Did you show her?" he asks.

I can't respond, because the truth is, I don't know how. I

turn away from him, running a hand down my face and trying to think of what I could do to show her I'm truly sorry I ever left her. I had to though. I couldn't let her be associated with me, knowing the cops would find out.

But they never did. It's the guilt that kept the distance between us.

"You left her, pushed her away?" Mark asks from behind me and I turn back around to face him.

"I had to," I tell him in response, but the words feel hollow. Even I notice the lack of conviction. If only I could go back.

"Maybe you should chase her then."

I don't think twice about it, not a second to waste. I shove my palms against the table and get the hell out of the room. "Talk to you soon," I tell Mark as I leave to go get Hally. When I glance at him as I open the door to leave, he gives me a nod although I'm not sure if it's an approving one. No one likes to root for someone who keeps secrets from them.

I don't need anyone's approval though. I only need Hally.

I have to take the elevator up to the fourteenth floor to the set she's on, while each second that passes pisses me off. The elevator has never moved so slowly before; the time teases me, taunts me really. As if it wants to torture me this one last time before I get to have her forever.

The hall's empty when I step out and I already know I'm going to be disappointed. I know something's off. I can feel it in the pit of my stomach.

The set's being taken apart as I walk past it. I keep going, straight to her dressing room. Slipping the phone from my pocket I check for a message from her, but there's nothing.

My heart stutters and my limbs go stiff; she's intentionally ignoring me, but I don't let it stop me. She's the one who wants to talk, and I can do that now. I only need one more chance.

I check her dressing room. It's empty.

I check her friend's, but it's vacant too.

Standing there numbly, I'm not sure what to do or where to go. I call her, but it doesn't ring, just goes straight to voicemail. I've never felt this alone.

It's not till I get to my dressing room and find the letter she left that I feel any sort of control.

Nathan,

I have to leave. It's the best thing for me at the moment. I'm sorry, but I have to take care of myself right now.

Hally

I stare at her signature for far too long, tracing the double Ls with the tip of my finger. She didn't sign it "yours" or "with love." There's no mention of us or where we stand. The only question on my mind is where I'm going to find her. Because if it's the last thing I do, I will find her.

Chapter 22

Harlow

There's something soothing about driving. Especially with no radio and the windows down. Even the city traffic wasn't bad. I kind of liked the sounds of the nightlife. As I head back to my hometown, it's all just white noise now.

It's not the kind of white noise that lulls babies to sleep though. My shoulders rise and my neck cracks as the weariness continues to run me down further into the depths of where I was years ago.

Alone and scared. Waiting every second for the cops to come for me. When I saw the news and saw his picture, it destroyed me. I couldn't even leave my room. I clung to a pillow, trying to will the memory to die. It haunted me and I deserved it. Every day that passed without me being arrested was a day I counted my blessings.

The guilt and shame built until I almost couldn't stand it. I wanted to beg Nathan to come with me and confess to the cops. I prayed to God every night for them to understand that it was an accident.

But no one ever came.

And the memories slowly faded.

Especially that summer, when Nathan was gone and the reminders lessened and grew fewer.

Even when I went back to school, somehow life became normal and sleep came back to me. The nightmares subsided and I became the person I once was.

That's a true crime. Living without repenting, and life is well with it all.

It's funny how the oddest thing would bring me back, and it would hurt even more. Because I'd moved on and never confessed. I swallow the thought; it scratches my dry throat on the way down.

My turn signal clicks and I look up to see that I'm at the intersection of Second Street where I should be turning. The drive went by so fast. My foot twitches on the brake, and the car rocks forward slightly at the stop sign. I need to take a right to go home, but that's not where I'm going.

My muscles tense and a voice in my head screams at me not to be so stupid. Not to go down here. The voice says I know better. The voice tells me it's all my fault for being so stupid.

The voice says I deserve this and I'll pay.

Funny how that gives me slight comfort. Or maybe it's just sad.

The streets don't look as scary as they once did. Maybe because they're empty. I huff a pathetic laugh at the thought. The boogeyman doesn't sit on the street corner; he hides in the shadows. My eyes flicker down the narrow alleyways, but I don't see anyone.

Goosebumps travel over my body as a chill makes its way slowly down my spine.

I don't even start to have second thoughts until I'm pulling into the church parking lot, parking under one of the three lights. To my right is the liquor store. It's still the same. It even has the same sign, although it's weathered now. Just a few blocks down is where it happened. But there's nowhere to park down there. Not that I want to.

None of it would have happened if I hadn't sneaked out that night to meet him at Nina's. It would have ended so much worse if Nathan hadn't come.

The sound of crickets fills the car. I never noticed them before. They're loud, but when I twist the keys in the ignition, turning it off, the sounds hesitate briefly then go back to chirping just as loudly as before.

Laying my head back, I finally try to think about what I need.

I just want to tell someone. I want someone to understand

that I didn't mean it.

I want Nathan to forgive me, rather than pretend like it didn't happen.

That's what hurts the most.

But even if he did forgive me, that wouldn't make it okay.

I'm lost and alone. And that's the worst feeling there ever is. It's the one Nathan chose for the both of us. *But I'm the one who chose it now.*

I have to tell him something, I don't know what though. Reaching into my bag, I feel around for my phone, but keep my eyes up and looking out of the window. A couple comes out of the liquor store, talking loudly and the sound of the crickets doesn't let up. It seems they don't mind the voices as they carry across the street. They're no danger so far away.

My phone lights up as I turn it on and see three missed calls from my mom. My finger hovers over the callback button, but I give in.

I don't have a plan and I know my mom will want me to come home. Not tonight though. I'll just spend one night by myself in a hotel somewhere or drive back to the city, although I'm already starting to feel the weight of the last few weeks settle down on me.

Just one more night to try to get my head on right. Although I may just have to drive all the way back. I left most of my stuff there anyway. Might as well.

"Harlow, baby." She picked up on the first ring. "How are

you doing, baby girl?" I hear my dad yell in the background, "Tell our star I'm so proud of her."

My voice hitches and I have to clear my throat as I talk into the phone. "I miss you, Mom," I answer honestly and tap my finger on the wheel as I tell her, "I'm coming home tomorrow and didn't want you to worry. I'm sorry I've been so busy."

"Harlow, baby. I just want you to come home."

"I don't know what I want right now," I say but add, "But I'll be home tomorrow. Promise."

"Well, you have time. Just do what makes you happy," my mom says easily and I wish it was only that easy. "I do–I have some questions," she says and I hear her voice waver.

"About what, Mom?" I ask her easily. As if I don't have a clue.

"About a boy. Ashleigh said you did date him, Nathan Hart?" my mom says as if it's a question.

"I did, Mom," I tell her and nod my head. I'm surprised my voice is so upbeat and that I can pretend it's alright.

"And what about now?" she asks me and I wish I had an answer for her. "The papers make it seem like--"

"The papers lie, Mom," I tell her quickly and a little agitation slips out. "Can I tell you all about it tomorrow?" I ask her and I feel like I'm lying to her because I already know some of it I won't tell her. And other bits I won't have answers to.

"Sure, baby," my mom says softly as if she knows how much I'm hurting.

"I love you, Mom," I tell her as my emotions start to

surface. "I have to go."

"I love you too, Harlow," she says but she's already lost my attention. A car screeches to a stop in the middle of the road and then reverses. I hang up with my mom, letting the phone fall to the seat before jamming the keys forward and starting my car.

My heart races. Stupid, stupid.

Frantically, I look back at the car as it pulls into the lot. Even though his face is a mix of anger and worry, everything inside me settles and I drop my hand to my lap.

It's Nathan. Even as he quickly parks the car and slams his door shut on his way to me, I don't have an ounce of fear in me.

I don't know how he found me, but he did.

Chapter 23

Nathan

"What the fuck are you doing here?" I practically scream as I rip the passenger side door open and slam it as I fall into the seat. She's got to be out of her mind.

She wasn't at her parents' house, or her aunt's on the other side of town. I thought maybe she'd go to the school. All Nancy said was that Hally wanted to go home. But I couldn't find her anywhere.

The last thing I thought as I went to drive by my old house, was that she'd be here. I was just retracing our steps from when we were kids, praying that's what she was doing too.

"Stop yelling at me and telling me what to do," Hally snaps at me the moment I look at her. My hands clench into fists and my jaw tightens as my teeth grind.

"You don't get to control me," she adds and then seems to settle down, but it's because she thinks she's won this round. And that's bullshit.

"You shouldn't be here," I tell her simply. I try not to make my words sound harsh. I try to say it like a statement, like a fact. She should know better.

I almost tell her those exact words, but it'll just set her off. So I wait. I hold my breath until she concedes.

"I know," she says after a moment and reaches behind her to put her cell phone in her purse, which is at my feet. "I was just leaving," she says as she turns to sit straight in her seat. She doesn't look at me and I get the impression she wants me to leave.

But I can't go that easy. I can't just let her walk away.

"Don't shut me out, Hally. I fuck up; I know I do. But I'm here and I want to be here. Please don't push me away. I can't take it again."

She seems to soften slightly, and I keep going. It's a sign that she's listening at least and I don't even know if I deserve that much.

"I have problems," I start to tell her and I don't know exactly how to say what I need to say, but I just keep going. "I don't have people in my life. I never really did except for you, and I know I do stupid shit." The words fall out of my mouth as if they're pushing each other to get out and go to her. Like everything in me has been waiting to tell her exactly how I feel. "I'm not good with words or with being there for people because I don't know how. But Hally, for you, with you, I want to do it all right. I want to be the man you need and deserve, and I refuse to be anything else."

Hally watches me, searching my expression for something, although I'm not sure what she's looking for. "I hope you believe me," I tell her. "You can talk, and I'll listen. We can start with that, and I'll learn. I promise I will."

I only stop speaking because she reaches out to me, putting her small hand against my cheek and I lean forward, wanting more of her touch. My lips graze her palm as she pulls away and I snatch her wrist, refusing to let her go until I can plant a kiss there.

My fingers loosen and I watch her as she withdraws again. My heart beats slowly, each thump noticeable until she answers me.

"Can we start now?" she asks me and for a moment I'm confused. "Can I ask you something?" she asks. I look out of the window at my car and then to the street. I'm tempted to tell her no, that we need to leave. But I can't tell her no.

I nod my head and she asks, "Do you ever think about it?"

"All the time," I answer her quickly and it's the truth. I'll never forget it. "The sound of," I pause to swallow before continuing and she interrupts.

"His head cracking," she says as she stares out of the windshield and looks at the brick wall of the church.

"No," I answer in a breath and she looks at me. "Of you crying out for help." I'll never forget how terrified she was. What almost happened to her will haunt me for the rest of my life.

She steadies her bottom lip in her teeth, refusing to cry as she turns away from me again.

"Talk to me," I tell her, reaching out and resting my hand on her thigh. "Please," I beg her.

"I wish you hadn't pushed me away. I needed someone, Nathan." Her admission makes me feel like less of a man. I only pray she can forgive me. It's all I need.

"I'm sorry, I'm so sorry I left you," I tell her as my eyes stare deeply into hers, the seriousness beneath the sincere vulnerability enough to paralyze me. "I'll never throw you away again."

I can tell it hurts her to hear what I'm telling her. She covers her face with her hands and lets the tears fall.

"I won't let you leave," I breathe the words. "Fight me, hate me, whatever you need ... Just don't stop loving me."

Her lips turn down and her forehead creases. "Nathan, you have no idea, do you?" she asks me and her words are filled with nothing but sadness. My heart doesn't beat until she finishes her thought. "I could never stop loving you. I just don't know how to make you happy. I don't know how to make us work."

That's all it takes for me to reach across the seat and wrap her in my arms. Everything feels right again when she holds me back. Her cheek rests against my shoulder as I whisper to her, "I've made so many mistakes, but pushing you away was my greatest sin."

I kiss her hair, her forehead, every inch of her that I can without letting her go.

"I love you, Hally, I always have. And I'll tell you every day." I run my hand over the back of my neck and throw my head back to mutter, "Twenty fucking times a day," before looking back into her beautiful blue eyes. "Whatever it takes for you to believe it."

She stares back at me without saying a word, just watching me spill every bit of truth to her that I have.

I whisper my greatest insecurity, "I can't lose you again."

Hally's hesitation kills me, every second making me exceedingly more nervous that this is the end.

"I don't think I'm cut out for this world," she tells me. "I don't want to risk my heart with you again. Not if it's just going to be shattered."

"Then we don't go back," I tell her quickly. Problem solved.

She stares at me with disbelief.

"We can go anywhere and do anything, Hally. You name it, and it's yours." It's really that easy for me. I'll live to make her happy. To keep her with me until the day we die.

"You really love me?" Hally asks me and I hate that she questions it.

"Of course I do. I mean it when I say I always have," I tell her, pushing the hair from her face. "I love you, Hally. I'll spend every day proving it to you if I have to."

The tips of her fingers glide down my forearm as she looks me in the eyes and says, "I love you, too." I already knew she did. What I don't know though, is if it's enough. If I'm enough.

"I just want you." The words are raw and full of nothing but the truth. "Don't leave me," I beg her again.

She closes her eyes and rests her head on my shoulder. "I promise I won't if you won't," she whispers.

"Then you're mine forever."

Chapter 24

Harlow

"Don't forget to smile," Nancy whispers as I prepare to head out of St. Gerard and back to normal life. Semi normal. As normal as it will ever be, I suppose.

All the footage is workable and unless Stevens calls us in for some extra shots, we should be able to take a nine-month break. At which point, we'll either have a season two or not. I think I'll be fine either way, but this isn't something I can see myself doing all the time. I think being an extra or taking on small roles is way more my thing. It's hard enough being attached to Nathan, the heartthrob of the big screen. I chuckle at my inward thought.

They can say whatever they want about him, but he's

mine. All mine, and I'm never giving him up.

"How could she not?" Nathan answers her, startling me and slinging one of my duffle bags over his shoulder.

"They could get those for you," Nancy suggests, her eyes wide as she realizes Nathan's carrying all of my bags and dragging his own suitcase behind him.

Nathan shrugs and says, "I've got them."

"Remember you have the Casitas tonight; it'll be a private interview in the back dining room," Nancy says as we all walk out of the doors of St. Gerard. The bellman holds the door wide open and the warmth of summer along with the sounds of the hectic city streets hit us both at once.

"Is that for Hally alone, or ...?"

"Both of you, of course. It'll be extremely important to mention each other from here on out to help promote the show," Nancy answers him and then licks her lips.

"Easy enough," Nathan replies and then nods to someone I don't see, slipping the bag off his shoulder and letting it sit on the cement.

"If anything changes," Nancy starts to say as Nathan wraps his heavy arm around my shoulder, "If you two get into a ..." Nancy continues, but she doesn't finish her uncomfortable sentence.

"It's not going to happen," Nathan says easily. There's so much confidence in his voice and it echoes exactly what I feel. There's nothing in this world that will tear me from him again.

A soft smile pulls at my lips as he looks down at me and then plants a small kiss on my nose.

A flash goes off behind me, and it makes me jump. I turn but don't see anyone at all. It's not until Nathan chuckles that I realize he must've set something up.

"Are you planting that one?" Nancy asks Nathan beneath her breath, a mischievous look on her face, but also something else—admiration, maybe?

"Mark's idea, not mine. I'll be taking Hally and hiding away with her every chance I get." Nancy nods, resigned to the fact that neither of us really want to be in the spotlight more than we have to. My hand slips into Nathan's at the thought of doing this once a year or more. It's hectic, but I love the hustle of it. I would never have thought my life would turn into this.

"I'm kind of going to miss it in here," I say aloud, although it really wasn't for either of them.

Nathan opens his mouth to say something, but at the same time our car pulls up to the curb and he reaches down to grab the bags. "We'll be back," he tells me and then starts to load up the car.

It makes my heart swell to know that I'll be leaving with him.

It doesn't matter what happened before. The sadness and pain will always be there. But if I can look at him and only see a man who loves me and who I love back, then we can survive it.

Even if it shattered us and the pieces will never be the same.

They can fit together and make something beautiful. Something it was meant to be from the very start.

"Well, I'm off," Nancy says and gives me a small hug. She holds me at arm's length as she adds, "You know my number if you need anything."

I nod my head and reply, "Of course."

She lets me go with an easy sigh. "Drive safely," she says and I know she's ready to leave until she has to check on me again.

"Thank you for everything," I tell her before she can turn away from me. "I really mean it," I say and try to put every ounce of conviction I have for her in those words.

She gives me a small smile as Nathan calls out, "We're ready to go."

"It was my pleasure," Nancy says and then she's off, fading into the crowds along the street. It's funny how life sets you up with people who will change your fate forever. How easily they come, but how they'll stay forever.

The driver opens my door as Nathan shuts his on the opposite side. It's one step off the curb until I'm tucked away and ready to go back to our hometown.

"I love you, Hally," Nathan tells me as I settle into the back of the car. The leather seats are cool and it makes me shiver.

"I love you, too."

I eye Nathan, taking in his words, the same that he told me last night and this morning.

"Are you going to say it all the time now?" I ask him teasingly more than anything.

"Yes, every second I have the chance so you'll never forget it." I don't know when he turned into this man, but I'm never letting him go.

Chapter 25

Lydia

Months later

The phone rings once and I glance to see who it is. Smiling, I let it ring, only picking up just before it goes to voicemail.

"Hello?" I answer innocently before settling down on my couch. My fingers trail along the dark blue velvet and I absently think about getting a new one. Not that I spend enough time in this NYC condo to justify it.

"How is my favorite shit stirrer-oh, I mean, starlet?" Joey jokes on the other end of the phone and my lips curl into a smile.

"Just getting comfy at home before heading out to visit a few friends."

"Oh?" she asks. "Any friends I want to know about?"

Page Six is calling. I don't do it for the cash, which is the sad part. So many people would be pissed if they found out it was me spilling the tea. But when push comes to shove, shit gets taken care of ... so I do the pushing.

"Of course you do," I say confidently as I rise from my seat and strut to the kitchen. This place is empty, which makes the large eat-in space with a twelve-foot slab of granite counter look ... lonesome. I ignore the feeling, turning my back on it as I walk to the floor-to-ceiling windows. "You want to know about all my friends," I tell Joey. And she does.

The line is quiet for a moment as I stare out of the fifty-story building, the tallest on this side of Central Park. The cars appear so small they're like the heads of pins and there's no noise at all. Just silence. I swallow thickly before replying. "I'll be meeting them soon and I'm sure I'll have something interesting to report," I say as I lean against the window.

I wasn't meant to be alone; I need to get out of here and move on to my next conquest. My phone beeps and I move it away from my ear, completely missing what Joey says to read what Harlow's sent.

I let out a laugh at the picture of them on the beach with the message, *Wish you were here!* I've never been happier for anyone else in my life. But damn, I miss her. It's not too often in this industry that you meet someone so genuine.

I text her back quickly, telling her that I miss her too and I truly wish I was with her. I let out an easy sigh, knowing I'll see them when they get back. "What was that Joey, I missed it."

"So, do you have anything for me or not?" she finally asks.

"I do." My lips twitch into a smile. "It might be a little bit of a lie though," I say, picking under my nails. "Only a little."

Epilogue

Harlow

PAGE SIX OF THE NEW YORK POST

A whirlwind romance on the set of Night Fire has lit more flames than anyone saw coming. The well-known bad boy, Nathan Hart, and the unknown darling, Harlow May, started a passionate affair that was more than obvious to director Blake Stevens. Capitalizing on the heat that sizzled between the two, the show itself was adapted to sneak in footage the famed director caught of the two while filming off set.

Reviewers and critics agree that the passion between the new couple is one for the big screen and can't wait for the premiere this fall. Even former costar Julie Rays has stated publically that she couldn't be happier for the duo and hopes to be at their wedding where she jokingly promised not to steal the show.

More scandalous than the affair on set is a picture captured of the pair on an island getaway in the south of France. Sporting a small baby bump and a ring on her finger, Miss Harlow May is sure to be Mrs. Hart before the year is up! Friends and family close to the couple swear the two are inseparable and couldn't be happier for the reclusive twosome.

Although the couple usually has no comment for the press, Mr. Hart responded to our request with a single line: "I lost her once, I won't lose her again."

"We're still making headlines," I tell Nathan from across the hotel suite's kitchen as my hand slips to my belly. "And apparently, I'm pregnant." The small smile that had graced my lips falls and I peer down below my bikini top. They can go get fucked, there's no way I actually look pregnant. We've been vacationing for almost a month now and it's time to get back to real life and everything that lies ahead for us, but I didn't relax *that* much. I may have gained five pounds, maximum. I half wonder if Nancy told them I was pregnant. She has a bet going with Mark, I know she does. The papers are calling them the matchmakers and soon-to-be godparents.

I squint at the photo, completely oblivious to Nathan's reaction.

"Are you serious?" he says and the disbelief makes me lower the computer screen. His dark eyes sparkle with a look I've never seen before, but it's one that makes my heart stutter, as if it's forgotten its natural rhythm simply because of the way he's looking at me.

My lips part and that smile comes back. "No," I tell him and turn my gaze back to the computer as the heat of a blush climbs up my chest. "I'm not pregnant."

Nathan takes a drink from a water bottle, the thin plastic crinkling and the sound filling the tense air between us. It's too soon. I keep telling him that and everyone else, the pain in my ass Lydia, especially. But watching his reaction stirs up something inside of me.

I watch the rough stubble on his jaw and throat move as he downs the water and then walks over to the recycling bin to toss the bottle.

"They didn't congratulate me when they asked for a quote," he says as the lid drops on the bin and he moves to the fridge for another water. "Those bastards," he adds jokingly and makes me laugh hard enough that my shoulders shake.

First comes love, then comes marriage, I think as I look down at my ring finger. A three-carat, cushion cut platinum engagement ring shines back at me. I'm still trying to get used to it, let alone the idea of a little one. It's just too fast. I pull my eyes away and look back to the article. *But we've never been a couple who've done a single thing slowly.*

My eyes flick from him to the words on the screen, not that I'm able to read another word. "Did you really tell them that?" I ask him.

I've never felt so loved in my life. I always knew I was meant for Nathan. I've never doubted it, even when he left.

He nods once and states, "I won't lose you again, Hally."

"You're so dramatic," I tell him half-jokingly, but we both know he's serious. And so am I. I know what it's like without him and I never want to feel it again.

I refuse to. He's my everything. And I won't settle on being anything less than his everything.

As I close the laptop, scooting it away from me on the slick glass tabletop and push my chair back across the kitchen floor, Nathan closes the space between us and leans against the kitchen table. He cups my cheek in his hand and leans forward to whisper against my lips, "I love you."

He presses his lips against mine for a sweet, chaste kiss that makes every inch of my body relax and melt into him. The moment he breaks it, far before I'm ready for the tender touch to end, I tell him words he already knows, "I love you, too."

About the Author

Thank you so much for reading my romances. I'm just a stay at home Mom and an avid reader turned Author and I couldn't be happier.

I hope you love my books as much as I do!

More by Willow Winters
www.willowwinterswrites.com/books

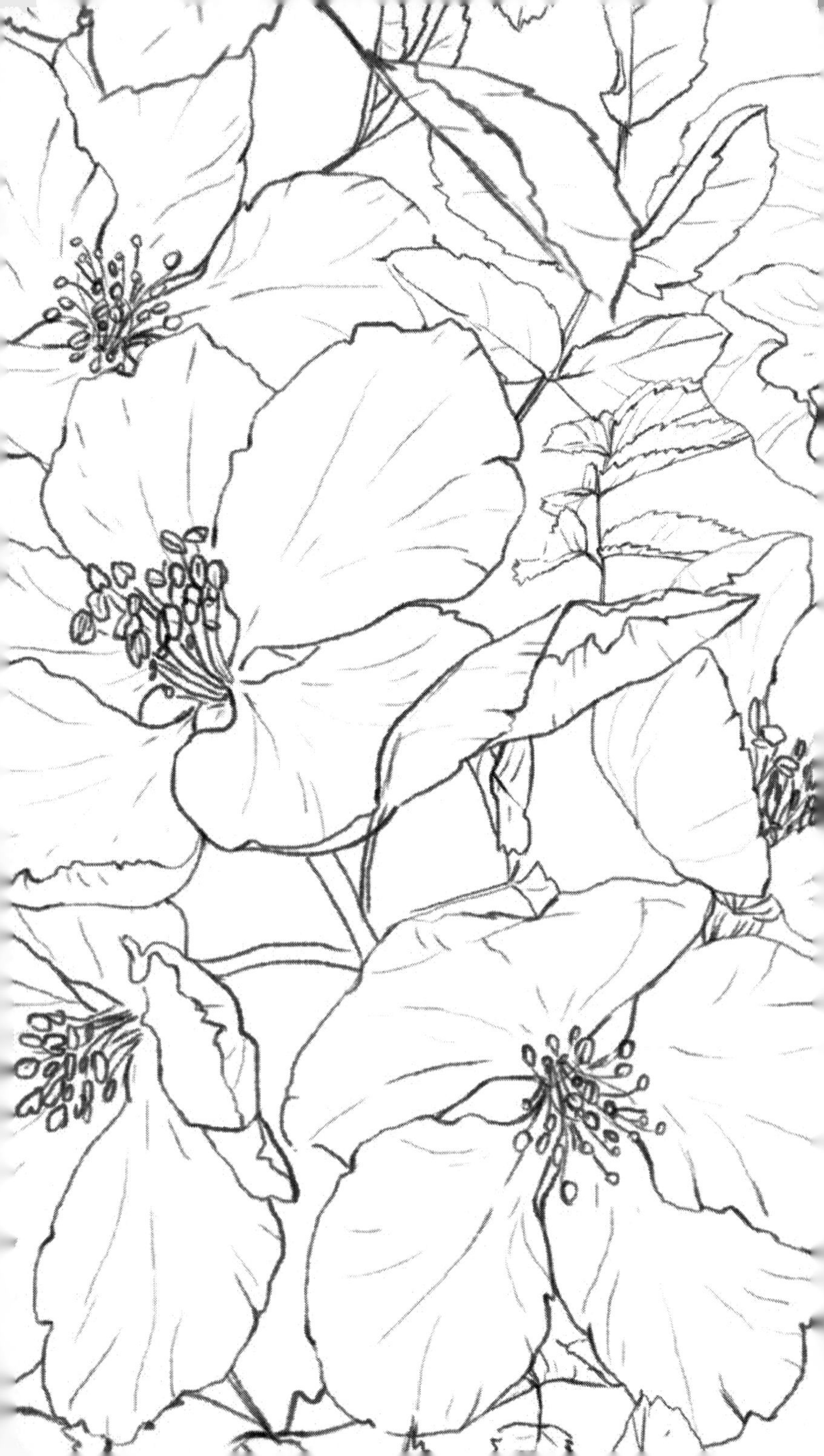

Made in the USA
Middletown, DE
24 June 2023